"It's All About That Money, Isn't It? You're Just Used To Getting Your Own Way."

"Wealth has its perks, I won't deny that. So, how am I doing? Convinced yet?"

She didn't say anything else for a few tense moments, moments during which they both, he was sure, readjusted the conversation to where all of this verbal foreplay was *really* heading.

When she finally spoke again, he knew they were both on the same page.

"I don't have a price, Sam," she warned him tightly.

"We all have a price, Ms. Halliday. It just isn't always money."

Dear Reader,

Did you ever wonder what you would do if something you wanted very much just fell in your lap as an anonymous gift? Would you keep it? Or, once you finally had what you thought you needed so much, would you look around and see that others need so much more, and begin to wonder if maybe you could manage without this "something" you had wanted so badly?

That's the dilemma facing Paige Halliday when a messenger brings her a letter that leads her to something she really wants, even needs. Does she keep it? Or does she pass it on to someone who needs it more?

For Paige, this is a fairly easy decision, in keeping with the way she lives her life. Her *real* problems begin when she realizes that it's the *messenger* she doesn't want to give away.

But that messenger, ridiculously wealthy, unbelievably handsome Sam Balfour, now has some problems of his own, and they all seem to revolve around Paige Halliday and the way the look, taste and feel of her seem to haunt his every waking moment.

Our anonymous "Santa Claus" had *no* idea what he was starting when he put these two together. Or did he?

I hope you enjoy *The Tycoon's Secret* as much as I enjoyed playing the "what if" game with Paige and Sam.

All the best!

Kasey Michaels

KASEY MICHAELS

THE TYCOON'S SECRET

Published by Silhouette Books

America's Publisher of Contemporary Romance

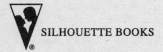

SILHOUETTE BOOKS

ISBN-13: 978-0-373-76910-0
ISBN-10: 0-373-76910-5

Recycling programs for this product may not exist in your area.

THE TYCOON'S SECRET

Books by Kasey Michaels

Silhouette Desire

The Tycoon's Secret #1910

HQN Books

Dial M for Mischief†
*Becket's Last Stand**
*Return of the Prodigal**
*A Reckless Beauty**
The Passion of an Angel
The Secrets of the Heart
The Bride of the Unicorn
*A Most Unsuitable Groom**
Everything's Coming Up Rosie
*Beware of Virtuous Women**
*The Dangerous Debutante**
*A Gentleman by Any Other Name**
Stuck in Shangri-La
Shall We Dance?
The Butler Did It

*A Beckets of Romney Marsh Novel
†A Sunshine Girls Caper

KASEY MICHAELS

is a *USA TODAY* bestselling author of more than 100 books. She has won a Romance Writers of America RITA® Award and a *Romantic Times BOOKreviews* Career Achievement Award for her historical romances set in the Regency era.

To everyone who pays it forward

One

The honor of your presence is required
At an undisclosed location,
December Twenty-fourth of this year,
At eight o'clock in the evening,
for a black-tie affair,
At which time an explanation
Concerning your anonymous gift
will be offered.
Enclosed are all pertinent travel
arrangements for both you and
One guest of your choosing.

Sam Balfour spared a last disinterested look at the words on the invitation and then lightly tossed it and a dozen others onto the large mahogany desktop.

S. Edward Balfour IV sat back in the burgundy leather chair that was two sizes too big for him now that the years had begun to shrink him, tented his fingers atop a generous belly and looked across the desk at his nephew. "You're making a point with that gesture, aren't you, son? Do I get three guesses now as to what that point might be?"

"No need for guessing. Let's just let these serve in lieu of a November progress report, why don't we? I'm sorry, *Santa,* but our fellow man is living down to my expectations again this year, rather than up to yours. Three good-hearted givers and fifteen bottom-feeding takers. I just got word that the last one, the youth counselor in Florida, took off for Vegas within three days of getting a cash gift. I warned you about cash gifts. Three, Uncle Ned, three out of eighteen. That's a new low."

"All right, I suppose I'll agree to accept that deviation from the usual monthly report. But please let me remind you, Sam, that the gift is always given with an accompanying note that instructs the recipient to do what he or she feels best."

"Right. And for most of them, what they feel *best* is to keep their good fortune to themselves, and the hell with everyone and everything else. Kind of like the guy who grabs his bread from the middle of the loaf—and then leaves the bag open so that the rest of the slices get stale. Hey, as long as I've got mine, who cares about anyone else, right?"

"And here I was going to add that I was wondering if that *new low,* as you call it, disappoints or delights you, Sam. But that would be only a rhetorical question, wouldn't it, son?"

"It doesn't matter what I think, Uncle Ned. That's not the point," Sam said, not liking the defensive tone of his own voice. "You've been doing this for nearly ten years now, and each year the numbers get worse. What's it going to take to convince you that people aren't what you'd like to believe them to be? By and large, we're a bunch of grasping, self-serving bastards, some of us putting a good face on for the world, sure, but all of us are really out for number one, and nobody else."

"And some of us may even be cynics," Uncle Ned said, his tone more amused than accusing as he sat forward in his chair once again. "I agree, Sam, that the responses to this year's gifts have been fairly disappointing. When I began this, more than half of the recipients took their gifts and turned them into something good, something that served others rather than merely themselves."

"Yeah, I know—considering the greater good over the individual benefit. Terrific in theory, lousy in practice."

"Not entirely. You said there were three."

Sam felt sorry for his uncle and employer. "Look, you gave it your best shot, Uncle Ned. But let's just send the three who passed the test their million bucks, have them sign their confidentiality agreements and put this project to rest, okay? No party this year. It's senseless. Unless you want to invite all the others as well and watch their faces as Bruce explains the rules and only three of them get checks."

"You'd enjoy that, wouldn't you?"

Sam shrugged. "Maybe. No. No, I don't think so. I mean, what's the point? As far as I'm concerned, the ones who react the way most of them do are the normal ones. Only an idiot gives away what he can keep. You know—don't look a gift horse in the mouth? You gave, they took. Why should any of them do anything differently?"

"Oh, Sam. You're breaking an old man's heart here. You really are."

Sam half sat on one corner of the large desk. "I'm only saying what I believe. Besides, Uncle Ned, I've shown you the articles in the newspapers. That dame, that Leticia Trent, she isn't giving up. Word is getting out on what you're doing."

"Yes, yes, I know. The reclusive billionaire Santa Claus who gives out unexpected gifts so he can watch what the lucky recipients do with them and then awards the generous with one million tax-free dollars in their Christmas stockings. It's rather shocking, how on the money she is with her stories. But it's only rumors so far, remember, no more than speculation. I'm not worried. I'm rather flattered, in fact, to be seen as some modern-day Kris Kringle." He patted his stomach. "I'm even working on the bowlful-of-jelly belly."

Then his uncle sobered. "This is what Maureen wanted, Sam. This is what she and I did those last few years before she was taken from me. This is her legacy. I'm not going to stop, not until the world has run out of good people, and I don't think it ever will."

"I understand. I'm sorry I brought it up," Sam said, reluctantly giving up the fight. Aunt Maureen had been bedridden for the last five years of her life, and the generous project had been her idea. She and Uncle Ned would scour the newspapers, the Internet, every day, looking for possible worthy recipients of unexpected gifts, be it the gift of money or something else of particular interest to the individual selected.

If the person kept what was given, used it selfishly, that person was out of the running for the larger gift at the Christmas Eve gathering. The initial gift would have been earned, as Maureen saw it, but no additional gift would be coming to these people.

Sam privately thought that Maureen and Uncle Ned were playing God with other people's lives, but he had always kept that opinion to himself. It was watching his uncle's generous heart being bruised year after year that made Sam want to see an end to the project.

Sam also knew his uncle's arguments for keeping the project going.

Uncle Ned had sworn that the searching, the

choosing, the anticipation, the joy when people they'd chosen had done such magnificent things with their gifts, had kept his beloved wife alive long past the predictions of her doctors.

Now maybe the project was doing the same for her husband, a thought that, when he admitted it to himself, scared the hell out of Sam. Because if Sam didn't believe in the goodness of man all that much, what he really hated was the *reclusive billionaire* part, as his uncle had been hiding from the world since the day Maureen died.

"Sam?"

"Yes, sir," Sam said, picking up the invitations that would not be sent this year, intending to toss them in the trash.

"You might want to hang on to one of those." His uncle opened the top center drawer and pulled out a dark green file folder. Sam knew the drill. Green, for *giving*. "I've selected one more recipient for you."

"You don't give up, do you?" Sam reluctantly took the folder. "Even if this one works out, Uncle Ned, you'd still only be four for nineteen. You wouldn't consider that a good return on your investment if these people were stocks or bonds."

"But that's the point, Sam. People can't be toted up on a balance sheet. People can't be assigned to the profit or loss columns of a ledger. I wish you understood that. You worry me, son. Your poor opinion of people in general worries me, as you've no good reason to hold such low opinions. Anyone would think you grew up in a hovel, downtrodden and oppressed in every way, rather than here, which I would think even you would say is the lap of luxury."

Sam smiled. "I know. I almost developed a speech impediment, trying to talk with that entire set of silver flatware in my mouth."

Uncle Ned tipped his head to one side and smiled at his nephew. "Did you ever consider that it might be the company you keep that's colored your judgment, inside and outside of your business dealings with some of the less than munificent of corporate leaders? Not that they aren't all beautiful women."

"They are that, and always in it for what they can get out of it—or out of me. Thankfully, they're also disposable and interchangeable, rather like the corporate leaders. But we'll leave psychoanalyzing my inappropriate response to being born with a silver spoon in my mouth for another time, okay?" Sam said, holding up the folder. "I'll take this to Bruce and get him started."

"No, Sam, you won't. There's been a change of plans. This one you'll handle yourself."

"Me? Uncle Ned, come on. I handle the paperwork, the gifts, the funds transfers. I take care of the invitations—all three of them this year. I arrange for the damn million-dollar checks and the Christmas Eve party. Bruce takes care of everything else, the meeting, the greeting, the hosting and most especially the delivering of the initial gifts and the follow-up. Not my job, not my table, you know?"

"You'll do what I tell you to do, Sam," his uncle said, his tone the one that had, in earlier years, been the terror of several boardrooms. "This one's local. You won't have to travel or lose any time from your busy schedule of running my companies and sleeping with any pretty woman with a pulse. Although that redhead last month would have tempted a rock."

Sam looked at his uncle in astonishment. "Pardon me? What was that? You're keeping tabs on *me* as well as your recipients? Wonderful. You'll have to excuse me now, so I can go find Bruce and break his nose for him."

"Leave Bruce alone. He only does what I tell him. Depressingly well in your case. I had to warn him not to bring me any more, shall I say, *interesting* photographs of you and your interchangeable and disposable young ladies. Frankly, I'm surprised they don't all have constant chest colds, the way they dress. You're my sole heir, Sam, my brother's child. I love you. But I don't like what I'm seeing. You're turning cold and perhaps even hard. You may well be on your way to being a *user,* and will end up a lonely, disillusioned old man."

"And here I thought you liked me," Sam complained, trying to deflect his uncle with humor. "I'm your namesake, remember? Raised at your knee, taught everything you know? I never realized I was such a sad disappointment to you."

"Don't fight me on this, Sam, because you won't win. You've known nothing but the cutthroat world of business, and you're very good at it. Well, and your ladies. According to Bruce, and those photographs that have been burned into my retinas, you're more than very good with them. In fact, I believe Bruce's last communication to me before I told him to stop included the words *he could give seminars.*"

"Well, thank you, Bruce." Sam grinned. "I'd still like to break his nose. After that, I may ask him for a few eight-by-tens."

"Smiling and being funny won't get you out of this, Sam. Humor me. Let me try to show you what Maureen showed me. I've sidelined Bruce and his camera."

"You're actually serious, aren't you?"

"Deadly serious. Beginning to end, Sam, *you* will handle this prospective millionaire. *You* will bring me all the reports. I don't know what will happen, although I've chosen this person very particularly and will admit that my hopes are high. I want to see if you'll have your bad opinion of your fellow humans reinforced, or if you'll begin to see what Maureen taught me to see—that the good in this world outnumbers the bad."

"But never outnumbers the greedy," Sam said under his breath on his way back to his own suite of offices in the immense Philadelphia mainline mansion.

He tossed the green folder on his desk, refusing to look at it, and went to lunch. He was pretty sure he was having *blonde* today....

While holding a phone to her ear, Paige Halliday frantically rummaged through a sheaf of notes on a desk piled six inches high with sliding stacks of papers.

"No, Claire, I'm sure I'm right. I just can't find my darn notes! *Ten* lords a-leaping. Not twelve. Twelve is... Damn, what's twelve, Claire? Oh, God, maybe you're right and I'm wrong. Where am I going to find a dozen lords a-leaping? I didn't think I could find ten. Are you sure? No, wait, I found my list, I've got it in front of me right now. It's twelve *drummers drumming*. Ten leaping lords. You got those? *Please* say you've got those. Yes, I'll hold."

Paige slumped against a corner of the desk, wondering why she'd so blithely said *sure, no problem* when her client had asked for a display of the Twelve Days of Christmas at the last minute, making the display a part of their mall-wide after-Christmas sales.

What were they planning? On the fifth day after Christmas my true love gave to me five golden rings—marked seventy percent below the normal sale price? On the ninth day after Christmas my true love gave to me—nine ladies dancing through the home goods department in search of January white sale bargains?

And all of the displays would be life-size, no less,

because the mall atrium was huge, and a smaller display would be dwarfed.

"Dwarfed," she grumbled to herself. "Dwarfs I've got in stock. It's the freaking eight maids a-milking that are going to kill me… Hello? Claire? No good on the lords a-leaping, huh? Okay, then how about— damn, Claire, someone's at the service door. Probably another delivery. I'll call you back, okay? Don't forget the four calling birds. No, I don't know what calling birds *look like*. What normal person *would* know that? Just wing it—ha! Get it? *Wing it*. Oh, hell. There goes the doorbell again. I'll call you back—gotta go."

Paige put down the cordless phone and jammed her hands against the sides of her head as the person at the delivery door had stopped leaning on the doorbell in exchange for banging on the door. Not that anything could muss her short pixie cut cap of black hair, but she hoped the pressure of her fingers against her temples might push her aching brain back into place.

She counted to three, dropped her hands to her sides and took a deep breath, letting it out slowly.

In the land of Paige Halliday, owner and operator of Holidays by Halliday, October was frantic and November was nuts. December was October and November put together, and then squared. The fact that the Christmas season brought her more than sixty percent of her yearly gross usually was enough to keep her moving, keep her functioning at the highest level.

But that didn't mean anything kept her *sane* between the day after Thanksgiving and December twenty-fourth, as the turkeys and cornucopias came down and the Santas and angels went up.

"Keep your shirt on out there, I'm coming as fast as I can!" she called out as she hastily worked her way between mounds of ribbon rolls and plastic crates filled with oversize Christmas balls piled everywhere she could find space for them. She sucked in her breath and her already-flat belly to edge between a grinning eight-foot-high snowman and a reindeer whose nose was *supposed* to be both red and electrified, but wasn't, and into the back room.

The knock came again, and she might have been a little bit careless as she pushed at the stack of corrugated boxes filled with loose silver glitter—loose because, after the reindeer fiasco, she'd already opened one box to check the contents. "Be right there—*damn!*"

She opened the door while picking bits of silver glitter from the tip of her tongue before closing her eyes and shaking her head, sending glitter showering from her hair, her face, her shoulders. She'd caught the box before it fell, but the contents had *sprinkled* on her a bit.

"There, that's better. Sorry about the delay in answering. So? How may I help you?" she asked, not really looking at the man who stood in the alleyway.

"That would depend," the man said, and the amusement in his decidedly sexy voice had Paige blinking the last of the glitter from her eyelashes and concentrating her attention on her visitor.

Well, would you look at that. Even the man's eyes smiled. Whew boy. Why did all the good ones show up when I look like an escapee from an institution for the terminally idiotic?

"That would depend on what?" she asked, once more brushing at the glitter on her shoulders. Silver dandruff. Wonderful.

"Are you Paige Halliday?"

"If I say no, will you come back in an hour, when I'm decent?" she asked him, wondering if his teeth were capped. If not, his children should go down on bended knees to thank him for such beautiful straight teeth. "Do you have a delivery for me? If there's a God, it's the pink artificial tree from Beekman's Supply. Green trees I've got in that garage behind you. White ones. Pink? Not so much."

"I'm sorry, no. No pink tree. It's starting to rain. May I come in?"

"I don't know…um…" She squinted at him. *Nice tie*. "Do I know you?"

"No, Ms. Halliday, you don't. Do I need a note of introduction from my mother?"

Paige felt her cheeks growing hot. "No, no, of course not. It's just…it's just that you don't look like a deliveryman, er, person."

"That's…very comforting, thank you."

Great. Now she was a master of understatement, of the obvious. The guy sure didn't look like a delivery…person. He looked like that perfectly mussed haircut had cost more than the down payment on her condo, his dark suit twice the value of her delivery vans. Tall, slim, handsome, he looked like money should ooze from his pores when lesser people can only sweat.

Still, Paige didn't know the man. "If you could tell me why you're here? I mean, if you're here to talk about decorating your home or business for the holidays, I'm open Monday through Friday. I even have a door on the main street, so you didn't have to come all the way around here into the alley."

"Nobody answered my knock on the front door. And it's after business hours," he said. "But I saw lights on inside, so I thought I'd take a chance. I'm harmless, Ms. Halliday, I promise. In fact, I'm the bearer of good news. And it's raining harder now."

"Oh, all right, all right, come on in," Paige said, backing away from the door. "Careful of that leaning tower of boxes over there. I don't think silver glitter would go too well with that suit."

"I agree. It looks much better on you."

"Uh…thanks." She turned to lead the way back into her workroom/office. "What's your name, anyway?"

She watched as he went nose-to-nose with the reindeer as he maneuvered his way toward the doorway. "Bru—that is, that reindeer is a real bruiser, isn't he? I'm Sam," he said, clearing the doorway.

Paige had caught the hesitation, the quick recovery. Still, she stuck out her hand. "Nice to meet you, Bru-sam."

He took it, his grip comfortably firm, his contact just a split second longer than maybe it should have been. His eyes, now that she was closer to him, were a lovely warm brown. And they were still smiling. "Just Sam, please. I tend to stammer when in the presence of a woman as beautiful as you, Ms. Halliday."

Paige was visibly deflated. "Oh, great. You're selling insurance, aren't you? Look, I'm perfectly happy with the coverage I've got, and I told the guy that when he called last week, okay?"

"I'm not selling insurance, Ms. Halliday," Sam said as he reached into his suit jacket's inside pocket and withdrew an expensive cream-colored envelope. "I'm here to give you something."

"Sure you are," Paige said, brushing at the silver sprinkles on her shoulder yet again. "Why, you're about the fifth person this week to stop by in the rain, just to *give* me something." She leaned back against the high worktable, wishing she had worn something classier than black jeans and an old Christmas-green angora sweater to work today.

"Is that so? Lucky you."

She had a feeling she wasn't making a great first impression. Especially since she couldn't seem to *shut up.* "Okay, look, Sam. I'm sorry, I really am. I'm not usually such a grouch, but I have these maids a-milking to find, not to mention the calling birds and the leaping lords, and I only have a couple more days to do that, let alone get them ready for prime time. You're not seeing me at my best."

Sam nodded, just as if he understood what she'd just said—and she barely understood what she was saying. "This is quite an operation you have here, Ms. Halliday," he said, looking around the room that should have been twice as big to fit in what she'd found a way to fit into it. "I think this is what is called controlled chaos."

"Only if the person saying that is being really, *really* polite. I'm hoping to expand into the empty building next door, after the holidays, but for now it's a bit of a squeeze in here. The rest of the year isn't this bad or this hectic."

She looked around the room, seeing it with his eyes, the eyes of an outsider, looking in. The tall topiary trees for either side of the Heckman's front door. The red and white striped pole with the Welcome Santa sign on it. Not to mention the seven swans a-swimming she'd already located.

Most especially not to mention that two of those swans looked like they were getting *way* too friendly with each other.

"Would you like to go next door to the cafe for a cup of coffee?" Paige asked brightly, trying to redirect Sam whatever-his-last-name-was away from the pseudocopulating fowl. "It can get kind of claustrophobic in here, and Joann's coffee is really good."

And maybe the sexy smell of your cologne will get lost in the other smells, and I wouldn't feel so much like jumping your bones.

But she didn't think it would be such a good idea to say that. It wasn't even a good idea to *think* that.

"A cup of coffee sounds very tempting, Ms. Halliday, but I'm afraid I have a dinner engagement in an hour, across town. I'm only here as a favor to a friend. So, if you wouldn't mind, I'd like to just hand you this envelope and be on my way. The letter inside, I understand, is self-explanatory."

"Oh." Paige stared nervously at the envelope but didn't attempt to take it from him. "All right. Um… thank you?"

"Not me, Ms. Halliday," he said, and suddenly the man didn't look quite as amused. "Believe me, I have nothing to do with this. Although delighted to meet you, I'm just the messenger."

"You don't look like a delivery guy or a messenger," she told him honestly. Was he flirting with her now? She was pretty sure he was, at least a little bit. Okay. What was good for the goose was good enough for the six geese a-laying, or something like that. She blinked several times, doing her best to look adorably flustered, as they said in romance novels. "So, no, Sam, I don't think I believe you."

He was staring at her now. Positively *staring* at her. Maybe she looked good in silver glitter? Who knew, it might be a whole new look for her.

"You should believe me, Ms. Halliday, because I'm telling you nothing but the truth. I'm the messenger. My... A client of mine felt he needed someone he could trust to take care of this matter for him. So I may be a messenger, yes, but I'm a very well-paid messenger."

Paige quickly shoved her hands behind her back as she panicked. "You're a lawyer, Sam? The person who sent you here is one of your clients, is that it? You did say a *client,* right? That's a summons, or something? I'm being sued?"

"Absolutely, not. Look, just take this and—"

"Not yet, no, thank you. Is this about the Gobble-Gobble for Dollars contest display in Bailey's Super-Shop? Hey, nobody got hurt, you know. It wasn't *that* big of a turkey, which is why it all happened in the first place. And it was only a blow-up plastic thing. How bad could that hurt? The kid shouldn't have been trying to ride it, right? Who tries to ride a turkey? And where the hell was his mother? She has to be equally culpable. That's the word, right? Culpable?"

"Gobble-Gobble contest? Turkey riding? I think you might lead a very interesting life, Ms. Halliday. I'm not a lawyer, no. But please do consider me sworn to secrecy as far as my client goes, even though I'm not a priest, either. No, definitely not a priest…"

He was looking her that way again. Why? She wasn't that *interesting*. Was she?

He stepped closer to her. "Hold still. One of those silver sparkles is very close to your eye. We need to get rid of it."

"We do?" Paige held her breath as he cupped her chin in his hand and used the index finger of his other hand to lightly stroke the skin beneath her right eye. He was so close to her, so intent on what he was doing. She could see little reddish flecks in his warm brown pupils. The slight laugh crinkles around the outside of his eyes.

She felt herself almost falling toward him.

Okay, so her body wasn't moving.

Her mind, however, had already jumped into bed with him and was ripping off his clothes with her teeth.

He continued to stroke her skin, out and over her cheek. His fingers trailed down her face, followed the line of her chin.

If either of them had a knife, there was enough tension in the air to give even a freshly sharpened blade a run for its money.

Paige swallowed and heard the sound of that swallow in her ears.

She was so…suave.

Sam smiled. Yes, all the way up to and including his eyes. "There, all done. You're safe now. For the moment, at least," he said as he stepped back, his neat double entendres circling fast and furious around her slightly muzzy head.

"Huh? Oh. Right. Er…thanks?"

"You're very welcome, but the pleasure was all mine." He lightly tapped the envelope just between her breasts, once, twice, and then held it there until she grabbed it from his hand. "It has been interesting, Ms. Halliday. Meeting you, that is. It's time for you to read your letter. But I think we must find a way to do this again sometime soon. For now, I'll find my own way out."

Paige quickly looked down at the envelope and at the way her name had been written on it in a dark, bold, definitely masculine script. "Uh-huh," she said, mentally saying goodbye to the handsome man who had to be the best-looking and best-dressed messenger in history, and hello to, well, she wouldn't know that until she opened the envelope, would she?

"Sam? Don't forget to watch out for the top box of glitter. Oh, and the door will lock automatically behind you."

Once she heard the heavy door close, she pulled a stool from beneath the worktable and eased herself onto it, so that her shaking legs didn't have to worry about supporting her.

What the hell had just happened?

Who *was* that masked man?

Most importantly—was she nuts? A stranger comes knocking on your door, and you open it, you let him in, you let him…touch you. You let yourself think about how *else* he might be able to touch you?

You even consider giving him detailed *directions* on where and how to touch you?

He had said they must find a way do this again. Soon, he'd said. She hoped he could find that way soon. She'd even be willing to offer to help him look.

"Well, this isn't good. I've really got to get out more. I'm beginning to have sexual fantasies, or something," Paige said out loud, fanning herself with the envelope until she remembered that, yes, she was holding an envelope.

She laid it on the worktable. It looked harmless enough. It wasn't going to jump up and bite her, for crying out loud.

She stared at the envelope until she thought she might be ready to read what was inside it, and then she picked it up, sliding loose the glued flap. Sam had told her to read the letter, so she'd read the letter.

Inside was one sheet of paper, typed. Unsigned.

Ms. Halliday, this communication is to inform you that a benefactor who wishes to remain anonymous has become aware of your continued outstanding good work with the Lark Summit Orphanage and wishes to reward your laudable volunteer spirit with a small token of appreciation.

Please contact the Sales Manager at Maintown Motors at your earliest convenience. What awaits you there is yours, to do with what you wish.

Be assured it is true, Ms. Halliday, that to give is more blessed than to receive.

"That's it? That's all? Give what? Receive what? That's *it?*" Paige turned the letter over, to find that, yes, that was indeed *it*. Just those few words. No other explanation.

The phone beside her rang, and Paige jumped, her mind immediately leaping to the idea that Sam was calling her, to explain the letter to her. She picked it up and pressed Talk.

"Sam? What does— Oh, hi, Claire. No, no, I wasn't expecting anyone else. Not really. You're kidding! You found the calling birds? That's wonderful." She slid off the stool, still looking at the letter, wishing for more words to appear, or to at least understand the few that were written there.

None did, so she put down the sheet of paper, the typed side facedown. She had more important things to think about right now. "Gee…that really is great. So, um, inquiring minds want to know, Claire—what *do* calling birds look like?"

Two

"I missed you at the dinner table, Sam," S. Edward Balfour said as he settled himself into his favorite chair in Sam's sprawling apartment in the west wing of Balfour Hall.

Sam never sat in that chair himself. It was his apartment but that was Uncle Ned's chair. It would always be Uncle Ned's chair, even after the old man was gone. "I'm sorry, Uncle Ned," Sam said now, closing the file he'd been looking at and placing it on the coffee table in front of him. "Time must have gotten away from me."

Too late, he realized that the file was still the same manila folder Uncle Ned had given him last week. The green one.

And Uncle Ned had noticed. Indicating the folder with a tip of his chin, he asked, "What have you got there? And why were you frowning when I walked in here?"

Sam picked up the short, fat glass he'd half filled with single malt an hour earlier and had yet to finish. "This? Nothing. Still a work in progress. I'll have the written report for you soon. So what did I miss? Please don't tell me Mrs. Clarkson made her famous spaghetti and meatballs. Except that I think she did, if that stain on the front of your shirt can be taken as a clue."

His uncle looked down at his shirtfront, which was curved over his belly, and laughed. "Soon I'll be forced to wear a bib, eh? As long as I kick off before I get to the adult diapers stage, I guess I can handle that. Yes, spaghetti and meatballs. It is Tuesday, you know, unless you've forgotten that, as well?"

"No," Sam said, smiling, "I hadn't forgotten." His uncle had very particular tastes, not to mention very limited tastes, which fit well with Mrs. Clarkson's obvious talent but equally limited repertoire of menus. In other words, if it's Tuesday, it must be spaghetti. "What brings you up here, Uncle Ned? Did you want to talk to me about something?"

His uncle's smile told Sam that he might as well forget trying to divert him, because there was no fooling the old man. There never had been—not in business and most definitely not in their personal lives. "Tell me about the girl."

At last, Sam took a swallow of the single malt. "Did you really call Bruce off, or am I just going to be telling you something you already know?"

"Bruce is on his way to Hawaii, for a well-deserved vacation. Your *face* is telling me at least some of what I know. I found another winner, didn't I?"

Sam slowly put down the glass and opened the folder. "I'm not as good with the camera as Bruce—I did get him to give me a couple of eight-by-tens, by the way, before I had him destroy every other photograph and negative while I watched. He loaned me his camera and telephoto lens, but I still felt like a voyeur. Anyway, here you go, minus the typed report," he said, pulling out a stack of photographs and lining the first few up across the front of the coffee table.

S. Edward levered himself up and out of the chair and walked over to the coffee table even as he pulled a pair of drugstore reading glasses from his shirt pocket. The man was worth two-point-six billion dollars as of the last quarterly report, but he liked drugstore glasses, so that's what he wore. He purchased them by the gross and had pairs shoved into drawers in every room in the mansion—a billionaire's idea of convenience *and* economy.

"Tell me what I'm looking at, Sam, please."

"You're just rubbing it in, aren't you, Uncle Ned? All right, I'll play your game." Sam pointed to the first photograph. "Our Ms. Halliday, arriving at the car dealership bright and early last Saturday morning, the day after I delivered the envelope. I had a feeling she's one of those bright and chipper in the morning types, so I was outside her condo early, hiding across the street in Mrs. Clarkson's car. The Mercedes doesn't quite blend with Ms. Halliday's neighborhood."

He moved his fingertip to the next photo and the next. "Ms. Halliday's mouth dropped open wide enough to see her tonsils while looking at the deluxe van with Holidays by Halliday painted on the sides…. Ms. Halliday stroking her company logo with something pretty close to awe…. It was almost embarrassing to watch her, as a matter of fact. As if I was invading her privacy as she gazed at her beloved. Well, you know what I mean."

"I have vague memories of what a loverlike look is, yes. Pity. Bruce would have gotten some nice close-ups of her face. He snaps a lot of film—click-click-click, you know? Then he gives me only the best shots. You're more the aim-carefully-and-shoot-once type, I think."

"Is that a comment on how I handle a camera or on me?"

"Ah-ah, touchy, touchy, Sam. Cut off her head on that one, didn't you? Maureen used to do that. We had to identify most of her photos by the shoes we were wearing at the time," Uncle Ned commented, inspecting the photograph. "But I suppose you did as well as you could. Your talents simply lie elsewhere, so don't worry about it. Go on. There are more, aren't there?"

"Thanks for overlooking my lousy camera skills, and yes, there are more shots," Sam said with absolutely no inflection in his tone before he handed his uncle the remainder of the photographs. "What you're looking at are shots of what happened after she was done crawling inside the van, sitting in the driver's seat—honking the horn a few times. She got out, stared at the damn thing for what had to be five full minutes. I think she might have been crying, but I'm not sure. Could have been the sun was reflecting off the van and getting into her eyes."

"How sweet. Pretty girl, isn't she? Maureen would think she had very nice posture. And then?" Uncle Ned asked, his eyes twinkling above the reading glasses as he shuffled to the next photograph.

"You know how to twist a knife, Uncle, I'll give you that one. And then she handed the keys back to the sales manager."

Uncle Ned looked up from the photographs, his grin as wide as his chubby cheeks would allow. "Did she now? Wonderful! And then what happened?"

"Right. Wonderful. And then I just sat there like a two-bit private eye waiting for someone's straying husband to slip back out of the by-the-hour motel he'd entered an hour earlier, camera at the ready and wondering why my uncle hates me."

"Poor, poor Sam. You lead such a hard life.

Continue. Ms. Halliday, as I see here, eventually re-appeared? Tell me—what's that she's driving?"

"Her old van," Sam said, barely able to unclench his teeth. What the hell was the matter with him? Why was he so angry with Paige Halliday for being a good person? Being a good person didn't make her any less bed-able, did it?

Uncle Ned was still looking at the photograph. "Ah, all right. Her *old* van, literally. So, the dealer-ship is going to deliver her new van?"

"Just keep looking through the photographs, will you? Or do you like shoving those bamboo strips up under my fingernails?"

"Touchy tonight, aren't you? Have some more scotch." Uncle Ned flipped through the remaining photographs, holding on to the last one. "You know, Sam, if I were the type to gloat, I'd be gloating right now. As it is, I'm just too happy to see that the or-phanage has a nice new van. But it's not the same one Ms. Halliday was looking at, is it? This one is longer and has windows. Talk to me, Sam."

"I got the details from your friend, the sales manager. Who, by the way, tried to hit me up for the cost of repainting the original van. Ms. Halliday, as you've probably figured out, traded the closed van you bought for her for a fifteen-passenger number she then donated to the orphanage. That includes an extended warranty, so said the manager, that she talked him into kicking in at no extra charge. As she explained to the sales manager, the kids often go on field trips and some other trips, and their current van is in the shop more than it's in running condition."

"Which very nearly describes the condition of Ms. Halliday's van, I would imagine?"

"If it doesn't, it should. The thing has to be ten years old." Sam got to his feet. He'd been turning over an idea in his head ever since he saw the orphanage kids riding off the grounds inside their new van. "So go ahead, crow all you want. You won, Uncle Ned. You found another winner. Another truly unselfish person is wandering around wide-eyed and gullible in the land of the grasping and greedy. Someone who actually believes it is more blessed to give than to receive. Now, it's *my* turn."

Uncle Ned was still looking at the photographs of the orphanage children. "Your turn? Your turn for what?"

For the first time in three days, Sam smiled with real humor. "I always arrange for the Christmas Eve party at some downtown hotel, correct? This year? This year, I have other plans. The party is going to be here, Uncle Ned, right in this house. And, if she isn't too busy sprinkling herself with fairy dust and separating copulating swans, I think I've found just the decorator to help me out."

"Here?" Uncle Ned paled, visibly paled. "But… but I'm not up to that, Sam. No, we can't do that.

We...uh...we haven't had guests at Balfour Hall for a long time."

"I know that, too," Sam said gently, aware that the last time more than he and Uncle Ned and the staff had been in the huge house had been the afternoon of Maureen's funeral. It was more than time to begin filling up the rooms again.

And there were so many of them.

Hell, a man could fly a kite just in the ornate banquet hall in the house Sam's great-great-grandfather had designed to be a miniature of the famed Biltmore House. Sam had been very impressed with the room as a child but mostly because of its great echo, not the hand carved stained oak paneling or the baronial-sized dining table.

And he had one distinct memory, at the age of seven, of taking a running start and sliding down that highly polished tabletop, doing fine until he crashed into a five-foot-high solid silver candelabra and ended up in the emergency room, getting a dozen stitches in the top of his head.

Who said rich kids never had any fun? It was rich adults who didn't get to slide down tables very often....

Sam shook off the past to concentrate on the present. "I think it's time we opened up the place. We haven't had so much as a Christmas tree in five years. I remember how the house and grounds looked during the holidays while I was growing up. And I've checked. Most of the decorations are still on the grounds."

"I should know better than to piss you off, shouldn't I?" Uncle Ned said wearily, collapsing into his chair once more. "No. I'm sorry, Sam. I can't do it. Not yet. The answer is no. I'm not ready."

"I didn't ask you if you were ready, Uncle Ned. I'm telling you what I'm doing. You do remember that you've already deeded your half of this beautiful monstrosity to me three years ago, for tax purposes? So, my house, my decision."

Sam knew he sounded hard, unfeeling, but he'd been giving his idea a lot of thought, and this wasn't some twisted way to see more of the frustratingly *nice* Paige Halliday. Not *all* of it, anyway. It was time his uncle returned to the world.

"Good thing I didn't gift you with my back teeth, or I'd be chewing with my gums right about now."

"Very funny. You don't have to come to the party, Uncle Ned. You've never done that before, in any case, either you or Aunt Maureen. I just want to have it here. If you think you *can* do it, that would be good, too."

"Which is what you're hoping for. You're a little transparent, Sam. In fact, I think I can see straight through you at the moment, all the way to your motives. Let me guess. You, not Bruce, will play host this year to the do-gooders, as you so cynically call them?"

"I will, although I'd prefer that you took on the role of host. And I don't mind being transparent, if it makes you realize how important it is to me that you… Well, it's just time, Uncle Ned, that's all. I worry about you.

Aunt Maureen would kick your butt if she knew how you've pulled back from the world."

"Leave your aunt out of this, if you don't mind. Even if you're right." Uncle Ned took a deep breath. "So all this for me, and the fact that Paige Halliday is quite a remarkably pretty young woman has nothing to do with any of this?"

"She doesn't," Sam said, feeling his jaw growing tight. "I can promise you that."

"So you say. This idea of yours is all due to some crazy scheme to get me up off my ass and back into the world?"

"I already said it did," Sam said, beginning to relax again.

"I know you did. And I believe you—about me, that is. But not about the girl. What I also don't believe is that the pretty little girl in those photographs deserves what you have planned for her. *I* didn't bargain for that. She's not in your league, Sam. She doesn't know the rules."

"You make me sound like some sleazy playboy out to collect another notch on his bedpost," Sam protested as he reached for his glass of scotch.

"No, I don't think you're sleazy," Uncle Ned said, smiling wanly. "And I don't think you're a playboy. You work too hard to be called a playboy. As for collecting those notches? You tell me, Sam. You're thirty-six. Why are you still acting like you're twenty-one and bedding women who just became legal, or something? Have you conquered so much in business that you need to keep searching for other conquests? Is it the chase that thrills you more than the capture?"

Sam drained the last of his single malt, not even tasting it. "How many sleepless nights have you spent trying to figure me out, Uncle Ned? Why do I do what I do? I don't know, Uncle Ned. I don't know."

"It wasn't because you had an unhappy childhood. Your parents loved you and they loved each other. Until the day my brother died, your mother looked at him with stars in her eyes. You're not emotionally scarred, you don't belong on a shrink's couch—at least I don't think you do. So why all the women, Sam, why the constant parade moving in and out of your life? Why don't you like women?"

"Hey, you saw the photographs. I'm extremely fond of women," Sam said, his smile crooked.

"All right. Let's talk about that. They might amuse you, for a while. But none of them lasts more than a few weeks, before you're off on the hunt again. Maybe that's the real question, Sam. You said your women are interchangeable and disposable. Obviously none of them is touching you in any way. So that's the question you need to ask yourself, son. What *are* you looking for?"

"Right now, a way out of this conversation," Sam said honestly. "If I promise again not to take aim at your little do-gooder, will you agree to my plan to have the dinner at Balfour Hall? Because the bottom line here, Uncle Ned, is that I don't want to upset you."

"Upset me? Now I'm fragile? I don't like that. All right, have your damn way, have the dinner here. Decorate the place, if that's what will make you happy." Uncle Ned got to his feet and handed the stack of photographs back to Sam. "But don't make promises unless you're sure you can keep them."

"No problem, Uncle Ned," Sam told his uncle as the man walked to the doorway. "She's not my type."

Uncle Ned stopped at the door and turned to look at Sam. "Apparently, no woman is. At thirty-six, Sam, if I were you, I'd start to worry about that. Seventy-five and alone comes soon enough. If you have nothing, no happiness to either hold or to look back on, I can imagine that seventy-five could be a pretty miserable experience."

Sam had no answer for that, so he merely nodded and waited for his uncle to leave before he moved to gather up the photographs and put them, and the green file, somewhere that he didn't have to look at them again for a while.

The photograph of Paige Halliday looking adoringly at her company logo painted on the side of the van seemed to stick to Sam's fingers. She was a beautiful woman, he had to admit that. Different.

When she'd opened the service door, spitting silver glitter, he'd thought her comical, uncaring or unaware of her beauty and extremely natural.

When she'd taken him into her workroom and stood beneath the harsh work lights, the glitter in her midnight-black hair, dusting the shoulders of the fuzzy green sweater that matched her eyes, sparkling against her creamy white skin, had made her look like some sort of Christmas spirit. A slightly naughty Christmas angel.

He wished he could get that image out of his head…but until he could, he was going to stick very close to Paige Halliday, to figure out *why* that image was still haunting him.

And one more thing…he probably was going to have to take at least a cursory look at the idea that, while he thought himself happy, even content with the way his life was going, his uncle seemed to think he should be miserable.

At ten o'clock on Wednesday morning, Paige Halliday stood in the alleyway behind Holidays by Halliday, a large blue plastic tarp spread out on the macadam, a painter's mask held to her nose and mouth as she carefully sprayed imitation snow onto a short, squat, too-pink-to-be-passable Christmas tree.

The idea was to tone down the pink, and she thought it was working. Well, it would be working, if the wind would just die down for a few minutes. As it was, she was getting a lot of the fake snow on herself and not the artificial tree. Good thing she'd taken the time to pull on the white coveralls her friend Bennie had given her last year, when she helped him paint his office down the street.

She bent down, keenly eyeing the bottom branches. Yes, that one needed another squirt, definitely. A little squirt here…another one just over there. One more quick shot on the lowest branch on this side of the tree. *Perfect.* Ah, the eye of the artist; it was a beautiful thing. She was the Michelangelo of pink Christmas trees…the da Vinci of artificial snow…the Picasso of—

"Is that offer of coffee still open?"

Paige stood up and turned around, all in one motion. The only thing she forgot to do was to take her finger off the spray can button. "Ohmigod, ohmigod!" she yelped when she saw what she'd done and who she'd done it to.

She tossed the can and face mask to the ground and all but leapt at Sam to keep him from trying to brush the puffy white artificial snow from his million-dollar suit. "No, no, don't do that! We have to let it dry. It'll brush right off once it's dry, I promise. I mean, I think it will. That's what it says on the directions, anyway. I'll pay for the dry cleaning. I'm *so* sorry—but you really shouldn't sneak up on people like that."

Sam held his hands up at his sides, like she was holding a gun on him or something. "You're right. This is entirely my own fault. What was I thinking?"

She blinked up at him, trying to gauge his smile

and tone. "Are you being sarcastic? Well, of course you are. And you're right. Who expects to be attacked by a spray can?"

"Not me, obviously. I wasn't sure it was you, at first. Who's Bennie?"

Paige was trying not to notice that the zigzag spray of puffy white on Sam's suit jacket pretty much looked like the Z mark of Zorro. But she wasn't sure he would appreciate the joke if she pointed that out. "I'm sorry? Bennie?"

"Yes, Bennie. Of Bennie's Bug Bombs. It's printed on the back of your…whatever it is you're wearing."

"Oh, Bennie. Right. Bennie gave me the coveralls. They're called coveralls. He's an exterminator, business and residential. But you've probably already guessed that." She tilted her head to one side. "Why are you here?"

"You had offered me a cup of coffee, remember?"

"I remember," Paige said, avoiding his eyes. His smiling eyes. His too-sexy-to-be-real eyes. "But that was Friday. Today's Wednesday. I didn't think you'd remembered. Hold still, this stuff dries fast. I'm pretty sure I can brush it off now."

"Thank you, I think I can manage. And you might not need the warning, because you're unarmed now, but there's someone standing behind you."

Paige frowned and then turned around to see one of her assistants standing behind her. "Oh, Paul, good. Hey, do you think you can put this tree back in the storage garage? It doesn't go out until to-morrow. Be careful, the bottom branches might still be damp in places."

"I'll be careful," the too-thin blond youth said. He was already holding both her mask and the spray can. "You've got some snow on your head."

"Of course I do. Why should my life be easy?" Paige muttered under her breath, quickly ruffling her short hair, hoping to dislodge whatever snow had landed there. "Thanks, Paul."

"Shall I meet you at the café?"

God, he's still here. Most men would have made a run for it by now. At least the sane ones.

"Sure!" Paige said brightly as she turned to him again. Too brightly. Nothing like advertising your desperation. "Sounds like a plan, Sam. Just give me five minutes to get out of these coveralls, and I'll meet you there. Go ahead and order. I take mine black. And I'd love a glazed donut, if Joann has any left. She probably doesn't. I already bought a half dozen this morning for my gang."

Without waiting for Sam's answer, Paige ducked into the building, already frantically stripping off the coveralls. "Mary Sue?" she called to her assistant, a chubby redheaded matron with the look of a weary soccer mom. "Where are you? Mary Sue—*help*. I've got to look drop-dead gorgeous, professional yet ap-proachable and maybe even reasonably adorable, and I've only got five minutes."

Three

Sam had taken a booth with a view of the front door stuck in the middle of two plate glass windows.

He saw Paige Halliday sort of skid to a halt from a full run, take a breath and then slowly walk the rest of the way to the door. She looked so elegant, sleek, tall and slim, her unusual short cap of black hair a definite turn-on, as were her deep-green eyes, long, swanlike neck and a tightly sculpted chin line.

Paige Halliday could be a top fashion model. It was difficult to believe she was also such a klutz. He was really looking forward to getting to know her better. Much better.

She opened the door, paused at the entrance and cast her eyes around the café, spotting him.

He lifted his hand slightly and waved to her.

Her answering smile threw a figurative uppercut to his solar plexus, and he got to his feet, waiting until she'd slid onto the facing banquette seat. "Black, just as you ordered," he said as he sat down again. "But they're out of glazed, so I ordered us each a slice of apple pie. I'm told it's the best apple pie this side of the Delaware. I have no idea what's on the other side of the Delaware, do you?"

"Last I looked, New Jersey." She took a sip of coffee, and then smiled. "But not *the* Delaware, as in the river. Joann meant Delaware Avenue. Her brother owns a café on the other side of Delaware, and the apple pie is from his recipe. So, technically…"

"Got it," Sam said, smiling. "I saw that you solved the problem of the pink Christmas tree."

"Look, about that," Paige said, folding her hands on the tabletop. "I really will pay to have your suit cleaned. How is it? Did the snow all turn to powder and brush off?"

"It's fine, the suit's fine." He'd left the jacket in the car to deal with later. "Don't worry about it. It was my fault for coming up behind you like that. Ms. Halliday, I would like to talk to you about—"

"Paige. Please call me Paige. I call you Sam. Of course, that's because I don't know your last name."

"Balfour. The full name is Sam Balfour. And why are you suddenly looking at me like that?"

"Because I know that name from somewhere. Balfour, Balfour." She leaned against the faded imitation leather back of the booth and stared at him. "Oh, wait a minute. Now I remember. Laurie. Laura Reed. You remember the name, Sam?"

Sam rifled through his mental filing cabinet and came up with a folder marked *Mistakes*. And there was Laura Reed's name, pretty close to the top of the list. "I might," he said carefully.

"You might? That's it? You *might?* She thought you were getting serious," Paige said, sitting forward once more, and picking up her fork. Although instead of using it to break off a piece of pie, she pointed it toward him, accusingly. "Choosing china patterns serious, as a matter of fact. She was my roommate our last year in college, and we still keep in touch once in a while. She's married now and expecting her second child."

Sam coughed into his fist. At least Paige and Laura weren't related. That could have been worse, even if this was still pretty bad. "That's nice. That she's married, I mean. It was a few years ago, Paige, but I don't remember ever leading Laura on, doing anything to make her think I might be serious."

"You took her to London with you for three days. Wined her, dined her in this castle you rented for the duration. I can see where she probably overreacted, read too much into the whole thing. The private jet, the intimate dinners, the diamond earrings? Shame on her for thinking she wasn't just a quick fling for you."

Sam searched for something to say and came up empty, which probably didn't matter, because clearly Paige wasn't finished.

"And then, when you only saw her one more time once you got back to Philly before dropping off the radar, not showing up for another two weeks or so, when she saw you coming out of a restaurant while pretty much chewing off the face of some willing blonde, I suppose she overreacted again?"

Sam closed his eyes, the memory of what had happened that night more than five years ago suddenly fresh in his mind. "I didn't press charges," he said quietly. And then he smiled. "It was a hell of a shiner, you know. Your friend packs a pretty strong punch."

"You think this is *funny?* Laura was heartbroken."

"Really," Sam said, beginning to relax, which was probably smarter than allowing himself to get angry. He remembered a lot about the beautiful, ambitious Laura Reed. She'd known the drill. She was chasing him to catch him, his name, his money. She'd gambled, and she'd lost. But she'd known the rules going in. That was Sam's policy; he only played with the ones who knew the rules.

The problem was, once in a while his judgment was a little off, and he came up against a sore loser. "And how long did poor, devastated Laura remain heartbroken?"

"She was married six months later. Chad's father owns his own investment bank, in Dallas, something to do with oil and gas," Paige said quietly and then looked at him accusingly. "But that's not the point. The point is, I *know* you. I know who and what you are, and you're nobody's messenger boy. So maybe you'd better tell me who sent you and why you came back."

Her eyes had gone a darker green, Sam noticed. Pretty, intriguing, but probably not good news for him. "As Bob Dylan said so well in one of his songs, 'you're gonna have to serve somebody,' Paige."

"I suppose that's true. I'll give you that one," she said, finally cutting into the pie with the side of her fork. Clearly the woman's appetite didn't suffer when she was confused or upset. "So tell me who you serve, Sam."

"Sorry, I can't do that. Why don't you tell me what was in that envelope?"

Her grin was so full of evil delight that he had to suck in a breath or else laugh out loud. "Sorry, I can't do that," she repeated right back at him. And then she lost her smile as she looked at him with narrowed eyelids. "You really don't know what was in that envelope?"

"Not until you tell me, no." It was either lie or involve his uncle, something he wouldn't do. Not now, when he was liking more and more the idea of grabbing that uncle by the lapels and pulling him back into life. At the moment, getting Paige Halliday into his bed was in the column Sam had marked *bonus*.

"Ah, but I'm not *going* to tell you," Paige said around a mouthful of pie. "Mmm, it's still a little warm. I forgot Joann was baking this morning. Quick, taste your pie."

He did as she said. "They're right," he said after he'd chewed and swallowed. "Best apple pie this side of Delaware. Why won't you tell me? Don't tell me my client is into something illegal."

Paige coughed into her fist and quickly reached for her cup of coffee. "Why…why would you say that?"

"No reason," Sam said, concentrating on his pie. "But, to be truthful, the least I can do is to assure you that my client is very upstanding. In his own way." Then he watched for her reaction.

"What's his way? No, don't. Never mind. I know who you are now, and I doubt that any client of yours is laundering money through me or something."

"How would he be laundering money?"

She rolled her eyes. "Well, I certainly don't know how. I don't even know what laundering money means, at least not exactly. Look, Sam, thanks for the pie, really. But you're not talking, and I'm not talking and I've still got to spray paint five hula hoops gold before five o'clock, so I've got to go."

Sam reached across the table to lay his hand on top of hers as she braced her palms on the tabletop, getting ready to slide out of the booth. "Don't go. Not yet. And don't worry, please. My client is the most honest man I know. Whatever his business with you,

I can promise you that it was entirely aboveboard, all right? But that's not why I'm here."

Paige subsided onto the imitation-leather cushion, but still looked ready to bolt. "It isn't?"

"No, it's not," Sam said, looking deeply into her eyes, his hand still on hers. "I'm going to be perfectly honest here, because I think that's what you'd want. I came back for you."

She pointedly extracted her hand from beneath his. "I'm not Laura."

"Good. I know where to find Lauras when I want them."

"That's really tacky," Paige said, shaking her head. "Not to mention insufferably arrogant, even if it's true."

"I know. I'm sorry, Paige. Let's just say I don't need my past misdeeds tossed in my face, all right? Especially when all you know is one side of the story."

"That's where you'd be wrong, Sam. I know both sides. Laura was out for the main chance, and you were more than happy to string her along so you could get what you wanted. Neither of you would have been up for saint of the year, and maybe you both got what you deserved. It's really none of my business. It's simply a life, and a lifestyle, that doesn't appeal to me. So thank you very much, I'm glad I bothered to wash the fake snow out of my hair, I'm almost flattered, it's nice to know that thirty isn't too over-the-hill to be hit on by handsome guys—but no, thanks. Now, once again, if you'll excuse me."

"I want to hire you to decorate my house and grounds for a small but elegant dinner party I'll be hosting Christmas Eve," Sam said quickly. "I'm also considering a large open house for New Year's Day, for friends and business associates, although that plan is still somewhat liquid."

"Really." Her tone told him she didn't believe him.

"Yes, Paige, really. It's been a long time since Balfour Hall has been dressed up for the holidays. As a bachelor, I haven't really thought about decorating the old homestead. I'm usually in the islands over the holidays."

"But not this year?"

"No, not this year. It turns out that I'm needed here. At any rate, most of the decorations have been in the family for generations, but it would take a more talented eye than mine, or anyone's on my domestic staff, to display everything to its best advantage. And then there are the trees—live, please, and at least five of them. And the live greens to decorate the staircases, the fireplaces. There are eight fireplaces in the downstairs, public areas of the house. I have some photographs of how it all looked years ago, and I hope you can re-create my childhood memories."

"I'm pretty sure I've seen pictures of Balfour Hall somewhere. It's huge. Photographs *would* help…"

Ah, she was weakening! Hit 'em where they live; that had always worked in business and in Sam's personal life. Diamonds for one, exotic locales for another—and, it would seem, Christmas decorations for one Ms. Paige Halliday. And Sam gets what he wants, just like he always does. Life was good…as long as Uncle Ned stopped making him feel like something was wrong with that life.

"I've got plenty of photographs. And then there's the exterior, of course. No blow-up Santas on the lawn, if you please. I'm thinking more of potted greenery and some discreet lighting. I know you're already busy with your pink trees and maids a-milking, but I believe I can make it worth your while to agree to the job. What do you say to fifty thousand dollars pure profit, in addition to any costs?"

"I'd say you're certifiable," Paige told him, sounding slightly breathless. "I'd…I'd have to hire an entire crew to take over all my current clients and then more for your job, as I'd have to spread my experienced people between the two. Even then, I'd be working at the house almost constantly if you want the decorations in place by even the middle of December. You should have contacted a designer months ago, Sam. A year ago!"

"My sincere apologies. And the extra crew costs would also, naturally, fall to me. Would you say that would run about another ten thousand?"

"Fifteen, easy. I don't cut hourly wages just because the people are only there as temporary Christmas help." She held up her hands. "No. Stop that. Stop throwing five-figure numbers around like that. You're not impressing me."

"Of course I am," Sam said, grinning. "Let's not play around anymore, Paige, all right? You're a businesswoman. You've probably already figured your profit and how you'll word the notice you'll put in the newspaper's want ads."

Her grin was self-deprecating. "Oh, I'm way ahead of you, Mr. Balfour. You forgot the phone calls I'd be placing to all the local magazines and newspapers, hoping for a photo spread. Visions of a national magazine four-page photomontage are already dancing in my head. My business would double."

"I could make a few calls, arrange that for you."

"God, you're smug. It's all that money, isn't it? You're just used to getting your own way."

"Wealth has its perks, I won't deny that. So, how am I doing? Convinced yet?"

She didn't say anything else for a few tense moments, moments during which they both, he was sure, readjusted the conversation to where all of this verbal foreplay was *really* heading.

When she finally spoke again, he knew they were both on the same page.

"I don't have a price, Sam," she warned him tightly.

"We all have a price, Ms. Halliday. It just isn't always money."

And then he went for the jugular. He had a feeling that his Ms. Halliday—he was already thinking of her as *his*—longed to be more creative than her commercial clients allowed her to be. A canvas like Balfour Hall would give her the perfect palette for some serious creativity. Nobody spends years and years in a design school for the chance to one day spray paint pink Christmas trees.

"Did I tell you that one of the trees I most remember from my youth wasn't a tree at all? Let me see if I can describe it for you. It was in the shape of a tree, yes, but it was made entirely out of enormous red poinsettia plants arranged in decreasing circles, to form a tree. There's a rather immense oriel window in the library, and the tree was always positioned in front of it. Incredibly striking, especially if there was snow on the grounds outside the window. That tree must have been fifteen feet high and half again as wide—or I was still quite small. Would you kncw how to re-create something like that?"

Paige nodded, not saying anything. She was, he was sure, already mentally figuring out how to build a poinsettia tree. He could almost hear the gears turning inside that pretty head.

"The banquet hall—sorry, but that is what we call it—will prove a bit of a challenge. It's three stories in the center of the house, behind the great foyer. Paneling, exposed beams, what you'd call an English gothic architecture, I suppose. My father used to joke that you could roast sinners on a spit in the fireplace. It's that huge, and I think he was right. That's where

I'd like to have the dinner party—in the banquet hall, not the fireplace. It will be a real challenge to make such an expansive space seem intimate. Maybe you're not up to that large of a project?"

She reacted to his last statement as if he'd physically slapped her. Her head went back, her chin went up and those fascinating green eyes narrowed once more. "Oh, please, don't dangle goodies and then try reverse psychology on me, Sam. *Mister* Balfour. You know damn well no designer would ever turn down a job like the one you're waving in front of me right now. If you let me invite photographers, the publicity could set Holidays by Halliday up for life, and you know that, too. I just don't know *why* you're doing the dangling."

Did she really want him to say the words? *Because I want to have sex with you. I want us to enjoy each other.* No, he didn't think so. She wasn't ready for that, not yet. Hinting, yes, but not anything quite so blunt.

"Do you really need to know? Or do you interrogate all your potential clients as to their reasons for hiring you?"

That seemed to stop her. She opened her mouth to say something and then seemed to reconsider. "No, I suppose not. Maybe I'm overreacting, or even flattering myself. I wish I didn't…. You made a much better first impression when I didn't know who you were, you know?"

"I understand. Give me Laura's address in Dallas. I'll send her flowers."

"Oh, yeah, that'd go over real big with Chad. Look, let's start over, okay?" She held out her right hand. "Hi, I'm Paige Halliday. I understand you're interested in hiring the services of Holidays by Halliday. How may I help you?"

Sam took her hand, and raised it to his lips and then held it there as he looked at her, as he lightly stroked across her knuckles with his thumb. "We could start with you coming to see my home. I could take you there, after we've had dinner tonight."

Once again, she withdrew her hand. "Oh, how smooth," she said sarcastically. "And now I know for sure, don't I? I want this job, Sam. Only an idiot would turn it down, but the price just went up. Fifty-five thousand, independent of paying for all materials and my crews," she said flatly. "And I have a feeling I'm going to earn every penny. You can pick me up next door at six. That should give me enough time to spray the hula hoops and hunt up a chastity belt."

He was barely on his feet when she was gone from the booth and on her way out of the café, waving to a gum-chewing blonde behind the counter as she went.

She'd certainly drawn the battle lines, thrown down the gauntlet or whatever else he could think of that might sound reasonable if he was standing in the middle of the Balfour banquet hall.

Sam gestured to the same blonde, to ask for the check and a refill on his coffee, and then sat in the booth, slowly finishing his slice of pie. It really was good apple pie.

His pursuit of Paige Halliday was turning into a very expensive project—he'd almost lost her over the Laura Reed debacle—but he also had a feeling that Paige Halliday would be worth every penny she'd earn.

For her decoration of Balfour Hall, that is. That's where she'd earn her money.

He'd think of convincing her to go to bed with him as a special Christmas present to himself....

"The van's all loaded with the last of it," Mary Sue said, leaning half into the minuscule office Paige had carved out in one corner of the workroom. "And you're sure you don't want to go along to drive us all crazy, positioning everything precisely?"

"Positive," Paige said, hitting the return key on her computer. "It's only a matter of assembling everything according to the plan. I trust you implicitly, Mary Sue, and it's mostly your design anyway. Did you remember the eggs? Six of them, for the geese a-laying. They're in the box on top of the worktable."

"Got 'em," her assistant said, peering toward the computer. "Whatcha doin'?"

"Nothing," Paige said as she turned in her desk chair, blocking the computer screen with her body.

"Were you able to make the deadline for the ad? I want it to run clear through the weekend."

"Also done. We'll be fine, honey. There's always a bunch of people looking to pick up some part-time holiday work," Mary Sue said, leaning to her left, again to try to see the computer screen. "That him? I was going to go next door to grab a cup of coffee and, you know, sneak a peek at him. All very discreet, and with him never even noticing me. But the darn phone wouldn't stop ringing. Move over. Let me see. Will he ruin me for all other men?"

Paige swiveled back to the computer screen and the photograph that had come up of Samuel Edward Balfour V. He was wearing a tuxedo and escorting a tall, willowy blonde down a flight of marble steps into what was probably a ballroom. "That's him," she admitted. "The picture might be a couple of years old, but he hasn't really changed much. Maybe he's a little harder around the edges now, but it looks good on him."

"And *this* is what you're telling me did everything but come right out and say he wants to jump your bones? Rich, handsome *and* eager? How long do you plan to hold out, hon? Five minutes? Ten? I'll talk to Paul and the others. We could start a pool."

"I didn't say he *definitely* wants to jump my bones, Mary Sue. It's only a theory. I think Sam Balfour sees all women as potential conquests," Paige protested, turning back to her assistant, whose smile was pretty much bordering on the lascivious. "And stop that. You look like a wolf eyeing up a tasty sheep."

"But I do love a juicy lamb chop. Okay, okay, don't frown, you'll get wrinkles and our sugar daddy might change his mind and take his business elsewhere. And you did so say he wants to jump your bones. Maybe not in those exact words, but that's what you meant."

"I don't know what I meant," Paige admitted honestly. "He throws around money like it's water— very expensive water. Except that, for him, he's using pocket change."

"A whole *lot* of pocket change. You must have really made a big-time impression on him, Paige. He doesn't look like the type who has to pay for it, even indirectly," Mary Sue said, grabbing her winter coat from the coatrack behind the door.

"No, I'm sure he doesn't. I don't know what he's doing, Mary Sue, I really don't. First the—well, never mind that, that's separate, or at least I hope so. Maybe he really does want to decorate his home sweet home, and the rest—that would be me, I think—is just a little added incentive. Who understands how rich people operate? Certainly not me."

"First the what?" Mary Sue turned up her collar as she looked carefully at her friend and boss. "Does this have anything to do with the van you gave to Lark Summit? Because I still don't get that one. We've got two vans, one not looking so good and the one that's on life support half the time. I like the orphanage, honey, I understand your connection there. But I don't get it. Why a van? And why now? Oh, and another biggie—why doesn't the purchase show up anywhere on our books? Because it doesn't. I checked."

"You might need these, and you're going to be late if you end up hitting rush hour traffic," Paige said, fishing the step–side keys out of the drawer and tossing them to Mary Sue.

"That's your answer? *No* answer?"

Paige gave it up. It was either that or just prolonging the agony, because Mary Sue wasn't going to stop until she had the whole story out of her. "The van was a gift, all right. Well, not that exact van. Another one. But I traded it in for the passenger van I gave to Lark Summit. And, no, I don't know who gave me the gift. It was…it was anonymous. To thank me for my work at Lark Summit."

"Damn, that was clear as mud."

Paige dug into the center drawer of her desk and pulled out the letter, still in its envelope. "Here. Now you know what I know."

Mary Sue took the single sheet of paper from the envelope and read the words. "Oh, wow. *To give is more blessed than to receive.* I think I see your problem. Somebody gave to you, and you figured the only *good* thing would be to give as *good* as you got. Am I right?"

"Something like that, I guess. I don't know. Maybe.

What's it called? Paying things forward? Somebody does something nice for you and you do something nice for somebody else? I just know that when I saw the van this person had given me, all I could think was that I have a van. Two. And the truck."

"None of which is exactly in the greatest shape anymore, and we've only budgeted to replace one of the vans next year. But go on. I'm listening. You saw the van *and…*?"

"I saw the van, and I remembered how bad the Lark Summit van is. Was. They were going to cancel the trip to Rockerfeller Center scheduled for next week, because they couldn't trust it on such a long trip. So I was thinking about that, and how much I loved going on day trips like that. Christmas isn't always the happiest time of year for orphans, you know? I mean, people show up, people donate gifts, but it's still not like having a family."

Paige lifted her hands rather helplessly and then let them drop into her lap. "I don't know, Mary Sue. I think I was in shock, a little, and my mind just kept whirling around and around. And the next thing I knew, I was talking the sales manager into a trade. I'm an idiot, right?"

"Not really. Sometimes you're just a little too good to be real, but you're not an idiot. So where does our handsome billionaire come into this? He delivered the envelope? Have I got that much right?"

Paige nodded. "We seemed to…we seemed to hit

it off, you know? There was some sort of spark, some sort of connection."

"Chemistry. Pure animal attraction. Got it. Loving it. Go on."

"He said he'd be back, or he'd have to see me again, something like that. But he didn't come back. Not until today. If I were a calculating woman, I'd say he stayed away just long enough for me to start feeling insecure, like maybe I'd overreacted, and then, when he showed up, I'd be really pleased to see him. Grateful, even."

"That would be pretty cold and calculated on his part," Mary Sue said, handing back the envelope. "Maybe you'd better rethink this decorating job. I know it's the sort of thing you've dreamt about doing. I know it will bump us right up there with the top designers in the city. But will it be worth the hassle?"

"He can hassle all day, for all I care. It's not like he's going to get what he wants. Not when I know what he wants."

"Really? But how much trouble is it going to be for you? Hang a ball on the Christmas tree, get chased around that tree by our handsome billionaire on the make, hang another ball on the Christmas tree? Sounds pretty nerve-racking, not to mention exhausting. I mean, unless you're only trying to convince yourself that you haven't already considered going to bed with him."

"Trust me here, Mary Sue, I'd already considered

that last Friday. No man has never had that instant an affect on me. It was wild," Paige admitted, sighing. "Now I'm not so sure. And there's still the van in there somewhere, you know? I really want to know how he's connected to that, because I don't get it. People don't just give other people things without wanting something in return."

"Sure they do. You just gave Lark Summit a new van."

"Yes, but I did get something from it. Personal satisfaction, I guess you'd say, even if that sounds hokey. It felt good, Mary Sue, watching the kids pile into that van. I felt really *good*."

"So maybe it made your anonymous Santa Claus feel good, too, giving you that van. How come you can feel good, giving, but you suspect the motives of someone else who just might want to feel good, too? That doesn't seem fair."

Paige shrugged. "Okay, point taken. But I don't think Sam Balfour is exactly Santa Claus. When he gives, he expects something in return."

"Like you, served up on a silver platter. He'll provide the platter."

"Exactly. Except that I don't think I'm worth all this intricate planning and chasing."

"No, you wouldn't, would you, honey? That's one of the things I like best about you. You haven't got a clue that you're a pretty unique and terrific person. See you tomorrow morning, all right? And if you think you won't remember everything that happens, for God's sake, take notes, because I'll be expecting a full report."

Four

"Here, try this now."

Paige looked at the vaguely round, segmented gray thing caught on the tines of Sam's fork. "What is it? And this time tell me before I'm chewing on it."

"You said you liked it," he reminded her.

"Yeah? Well, that was before you told me it was a mussel. I don't eat mussels."

"You do now. You asked me for another one. Now, come on, be daring. Open up."

She looked at the whatever-it-was a second time and then closed her eyes and opened her mouth, closing it again around the tines of the fork. Her eyes opened wide as the spiciness of whatever the whatever-it-was had been marinated in hit her taste buds with the impact only slightly less powerful than being slapped upside the head with a two-by-four.

She swallowed without chewing, even as she grabbed her water glass and drank deeply. Even the inside of her lips were on fire. She could feel little beads of perspiration forming under her eyes and wiped at them with her napkin. "Admit it, you're a sadist, aren't you? What…what *was* that?"

Sam looked entirely too happy, so she was pretty sure she wasn't going to like his answer.

"Squid. Marinated squid. So?"

"Oh, *yuck*. So now I understand why they soaked it in cayenne pepper. It was so a person doesn't have to taste it. How can you eat that stuff?"

"It's considered very *avant-garde* in some circles, I believe. A true seafood medley salad. Although you're probably right. Mostly, it's greens and spices. But, congratulations for being so willing to try something new. You're very daring."

"I learned fairly early to eat what's put in front of me. But I think I just hit the wall on that one. I'll stick to my French onion soup from here on out, okay?"

"So that rules out the octopus I was going to offer you next?"

"I think that would be a safe deduction, yes." Paige looked across the large yet strangely intimate dining room. Every table was occupied, and it was only Wednesday night. She wished yet again that she'd had time to go home, to shower and put on another outfit, but she couldn't spend time worrying about what couldn't be changed. "I've never been here before. It's a very lovely restaurant."

"Thank you. I suppose I should tell you that I own it," Sam said, lifting his wineglass to his lips.

"Well, then, how very *lovely* for you," Paige said as the waiter removed the soup bowl and replaced it with her entrée. Why on earth had she ordered lamb chops?

"I had no choice. Bertran's is one of the premier restaurants in the city. It was either buy it or take the chance of not being able to get a reservation."

"Yes, I see the logic," Paige said, trying hard to keep a straight face. She couldn't do it. "It must be terrific fun to be so filthy rich. You probably giggle all the time."

Sam leaned his chin in his hand as he and his wonderful brown eyes smiled at her across the table. "You have no idea. But being filthy rich does come with certain drawbacks."

"The Laura Reeds of this world," Paige said, knowing where he was going, although she didn't know why she knew. It seemed as if they could say only a few words to each other, yet know exactly what the other person meant, where the conversation was headed next. It was almost…spooky.

"Yes, the Laura Reeds of this world. Beautiful women throwing themselves at me, day in, day out. It's a burden I carry."

"Because you don't know if they're throwing themselves at you or at your money."

"Oh, it's the money, Paige. I have no illusions there. I've learned to dread the day the *Fortune 300* is published every year."

"But you're also very handsome. And even nice, when you want to be."

"Why, thank you, Ms. Halliday." He sat back in his chair, feigning embarrassment. "Am I blushing?"

"Stop that. I'm not saying anything you don't already know. No man walks the way you do, dresses the way you do, without knowing the impact he's making on women."

Sam put a hand to his chest as he looked down at his clothing. "It's just a suit, Paige. All businessmen wear suits."

"Not the way you wear them," she said, wishing she could shut up. But this was fun, this back and forth. "And the hair? Just mussed enough to know that it was cut to look just the way it does."

"Oh? And how does it look?"

She swallowed her first bite of perfectly grilled lamb chop, praying she wouldn't choke on it. "Like you just got out of bed. Like you'd be more than willing to go back to bed, with the right company. Oh, God, did I just say that?"

"You did. Looks like I'm going to have to buy my hair salon now, too. I like your hair, you know. There aren't many women with the bone structure to wear their hair so short. Although I might miss the silver glitter, just a little bit."

She looked at him, unable to look away. His eyes smiled into hers, and her stomach did a small flip.

Paige dipped her head, to concentrate on her plate. "This lamb chop is huge but really delicious. You're not eating."

"I'd say I was feasting on you, but then I'd have to shoot myself for being so corny."

She smiled, relaxing again. "And I'd have to cock the pistol for you. That was really bad. Lame, actually."

"I know. Sorry," he said, slicing into his New York strip steak. "I usually don't order red meat when I'm out with a woman, but you gave me hope when you ordered the lamb. You don't mind that I'm a carnivore? No lectures coming my way, on either my clogging arteries or cruelty to animals?"

"Not from me. I'm a simple person, happy with meat and potatoes, neither of which I have time to cook very often. If I were home right now, I'd probably be eating a peanut-butter-and-jelly sandwich over the sink. Jelly drips, if you use enough of it, and I do—and on unhealthy white bread, which is the only way to eat PB and J. So, personally, Sam? No, I don't care if you march an entire cow in here and take a bite out of it."

Once again, Sam leaned forward, his chin in his hand. "Ah, this is interesting. I don't believe I can remember having such an honest conversation with a woman. Truthfully, I don't remember the last time I sat across a dinner table and watched any woman eat more than a few bites of anything."

"And, ignoring the fact that I obviously don't eat like an undernourished canary, that makes me wonder what sort of conversations you do have with women. Politics, global warming, the latest Hollywood gossip—the best place to have your Rolls Royce detailed?"

"I don't think the women I see would be interested in any of that. Mostly, they ask questions. 'Do you like my dress? Does my hair look all right?'" His grin widened. "Later in the evening, it's more like, 'Don't wrinkle my dress…. Be careful of my hair.'"

"Really? Well, you won't hear any of that from me," Paige warned him, and then caught herself. The man was maddening! He was only teasing her, and she knew it, but for some stupid, unexplainable reason, he was also beginning to turn her on. It *had* been a long time between turn-ons, apparently. "I mean…because the…the situation wouldn't arise."

"Never say never, Paige," Sam told her. "I know I never do. But let's get back to our discussion. The man in your life would be trusted to make his own diet choices?"

Paige relaxed yet again. "Mostly. Although I'd probably make him swear off squid or else never kiss me. My lips are still burning."

"Point taken. Let's pursue this, all right? Drawing

from my memory of complaints I've heard from some of my married friends, how many rounds of golf is a reasonable number for the man in your life? Per week."

"The *hypothetical* man in my life," Paige was careful to clarify. "You play golf?"

"No, it's just a question. Yes, I play golf. Do you?"

"Only the kind where you have to hit between the rotating blades of a windmill, or get the ball into the lion's mouth. But I'm very good. Three."

"Three what? Oh, three times a week. That seems reasonable. What about sex?"

This time Paige did choke, a little. "You asked me about golf *before* you asked me about sex?"

His eyes were all but dancing in his head. "A man needs to keep his priorities straight."

"You apparently *do* talk to a lot of married men, to say that." Paige pretended to give his silly question serious consideration. "Okay, I've got a number. Once a day, I imagine."

"All right then, good enough, that takes care of days," Sam teased. "And how many nights?"

She looked at him sternly. "You know what I meant, Sam. To clarify, I meant once in every twenty-four hour period. Or was that question meant as just a sly way of bragging? Because I'm not impressed."

"Damn. I keep working my way up to a full count, and then I strike out again. Tell me, Paige, how do I get to first base?"

Paige popped a small oven-roasted potato into her

mouth and chewed on it for a while before she swallowed it, delaying her answer. He watched her closely, as if truly interested in what she would say next. So she told him the truth. "Persistence?"

She watched as his left eyebrow rose slightly, giving his handsome face a rakish look, rather like a clean-cut Jack Sparrow as played by Johnny Depp in *Pirates of the Caribbean*. She reached for her wine glass to cover her sudden nervousness.

Sam lifted his own glass and held it out toward hers. "A toast then, to persistence."

It was after nine when Sam drove through the gates and up the long, curving drive to Balfour Hall. His uncle went to bed at nine. A person could set his watch by Uncle Ned's bedtime habits, so there were no lights showing in the second floor of the east wing.

Beside Sam on the front seat, Paige was leaning forward, her eyes wide. "The photographs I've seen don't come close to showing how massive this place is," she said in some awe. "You grew up here? I'll bet hide-and-seek was a bunch of fun. Unless you starved to death before anybody found you."

"I'm an only child, Paige. I didn't get to play hide-and-seek. Just hide, which I was extremely good at, by the way. But I had a pony, so maybe we can consider it a draw?"

"More than a draw. A pony trumps just about anything else I can think of. What was his name?"

"*Her* name was Susie." Sam pulled the car into the circular area of the drive, parking it in front of the door. "I haven't thought about Susie in years. We still have the stables, but there hasn't been a horse in them for a long, long time."

She didn't wait for him to walk around to her side of the car, but was standing on the drive, waiting for him. "How much land do you have here, Sam? Obviously enough to keep your own horses. I didn't think anyone owned that much land this close to the city, not anymore."

"The original Balfour was a farmer way back in the seventeen-hundreds, which explains the amount of land, I suppose, and a descendant didn't much like farming but discovered that he was a whiz at figures, which explains the house and fortune. I've never really thought about it much, which probably makes me shallow and unappreciative. I've just never known anything but this house, this way of life. Come on, it's getting cold. Let's go inside."

He slipped his arm around her shoulders and led her up the wide steps to the massive front doors.

"If you ring the bell, will an English butler in an old-fashioned tuxedo open the door? And do you think I could ask any more stupid questions before I learn to keep my mouth shut? I should have stopped at one glass of wine."

Sam smiled as he slipped a key in the lock and ushered her into the massive foyer. "You didn't finish the second glass, and I like your questions. Most people try so hard to look bored and unimpressed that it's obvious they're just dying to gawk and stare. So go for it, Paige. Be it ever so humble, there's no place like a mansion."

She didn't have to be asked twice, it seemed, as she walked into the center of the foyer that was really more of an enormous marble-floored room, complete with fireplace and a double set of curving, ornately carved wooden staircases that climbed the side walls and met in a gallery more than thirty feet wide.

If he looked at the great foyer through her eyes, as he found he was doing now, he would have to say he was pretty damn impressed himself. Funny how a person doesn't notice what's always just, well, just been there for all of his thirty-six years.

She turned in a circle, her head tipped back, looking up at the chandelier, an eight-foot-high mass of rubbed brass and crystal prisms hanging high above a parquet wood round table currently holding a large vase filled with hothouse flowers.

"Someone changes those flowers every week, I think," he told her. "Different vases, different flowers. It used to make me feel like I was living in a hotel. You can either have the florist take care of that or do something of your own for the table."

"Every week? I guess that beats the hell out of a bunch of silk flowers picked up on sale at the local hobby shop and then just changed out with the seasons," Paige said, still turning in slow circles. "Not that you'd know that, of course."

He had to say one thing for Paige Halliday. She didn't watch every word she said around him, was obviously not out to impress him. He liked that. "Sorry. I've lived a deprived life."

"Uh-huh, sure. Do you think you have ladders anywhere? I don't think I own any long enough to reach that chandelier, and I'd kill to decorate it." She stopped moving around and looked at him. "You said you have photographs. I'd love to see them. See what was done with these fantastic staircases. I mean, I have some ideas, but I'd rather stick with tradition as much as possible."

"Why don't we finish the tour first and then look at the photographs." Sam motioned for her to follow him through the archway to the left of the foyer, and into the first public reception room. The baseboards and wainscoting were painted a creamy ivory, the walls above the wainscoting a deep maroon, the furniture plentiful, massive and overstuffed. Uncle Ned called it the main saloon. Sam's mother, when she'd wanted to tease her brother-in-law, called the room the Bordello Reception Parlor.

Sam smiled at the memory. He didn't even remember the last time he'd been in this room, let alone thought of his mother's old joke.

Now he was seeing the foyer, the drawing room,

which they entered next, and the other rooms they walked through, through Paige's eyes. Her eyes were filled with wonderment, and she was not too proud to show her delight or too jaded to realize that Balfour Hall was a treasure trove of things to see, to marvel at and enjoy.

These were the public rooms, those built and maintained entirely for show, to host the huge parties, celebrations and even charity balls that once had been so much a part of Balfour Hall.

Now they were just pretty rooms, filled with furniture, with fine art and priceless antiques collected by Balfours for several generations. But they also were rooms more dead than alive, like the silk flowers Paige mentioned, and not *real* anymore.

Somehow, without even trying, Paige was making them come alive again.

For the most part, Uncle Ned lived in a few rooms, which were more than sufficient for his needs. Sam had his wing, the wing that had been his parents' before him—before his father's sudden death, before his mother pulled herself together and moved to their winter home in Sarasota, to try to pick up the pieces of her life.

He'd actually had to hunt up the key to the front door before meeting Paige for dinner, because he usually entered directly into his own wing.

Sam heard a small voice in his brain, asking him a question, one dripping with sarcasm, or maybe tinged with regret: *Welcome home, Sam. Where the hell have you been?*

They were in the library now, and Paige was looking at the life-size portrait above the fireplace. "You look like him. Are those your parents?"

Sam stepped closer, looking up at the portrait. "You know, I'd never noticed a resemblance. You really think I look like him? He was probably about my age when this was painted."

"Oh, yes, definitely. I mean, not *exactly* like him. But there's something about the eyes. Your eyes smile, did you know that?"

"That's the devil peeking out of them," Sam told her. "At least my mother swears that's who it is. Both with my father and with me. He's been gone for a while now. He died unexpectedly only a few months after I'd finished grad school. One day he was diagnosed, and two weeks later it was all over. My mother lives in Florida now. She said she couldn't stand to stay here, without him."

"I'm sorry. It must hurt so much, to lose a parent."

"It isn't easy, no." Sam took Paige's hand and walked her toward the enormous oriel window that looked out over the grounds. "This is the window I told you about."

"Where you want the poinsettia tree, yes. It's going to be magnificent. I can up-light it at night. It's terrific that this window faces the front of the house. The tree will make a definite statement."

"It sure will. Hey, look, it'll say—big red tree!"

"Don't mock me. I could use pink poinsettias and spray snow on them." She looked at him. "But I really want to see this banquet hall for millions that I'm supposed to make intimate enough for a small dinner party. And then I'm going to need a chair and another glass of wine, because I think I'm going to have a small nervous breakdown. This is a *huge* job, Sam."

"I trust you. Come on, the banquet hall is this way," he said, taking her hand, which felt good, which felt natural. He was going to have to give this whole thing more thought. The woman was beginning to get to him. He hadn't expected that. In matters of romance, it was usually the other way around. And if Sam knew one thing about himself, it was that he needed to be the one in control.

They walked back to the great foyer by way of the morning room, the sitting room, passing by the short hallway to the family dining room, all while Paige marveled at the decorated ceilings, the distinctive fireplaces that, in most cases, had been imported from bankrupt estates in England and France when Balfour Hall was built.

He showed her the pianoforte in the music room, an antique supposedly once used by Mozart to entertain guests during some English country house party.

"That harp in the corner looks pretty old," Paige commented. "Is there a story behind that, too?"

Sam smiled. "There is, yes. A cautionary tale, one filled with warnings about what happens to little boys when they try to stick their head between the strings. I nearly sliced off an ear. A house like this can make for a dangerous playground for little boys on rainy days."

"I can't even imagine growing up as the only child in a house this large and ornate," Paige told him, squeezing his hand. The gesture seemed natural, not planned. "You were lonely?"

"No, although I could lie and try to play on your sympathies by telling you what a poor little rich boy I was. What I was, Paige, was hell on wheels."

"*Was?* As in the past tense?"

"Oh, yes. I'm much better now." He stopped in front of the pair of thickly carved doors more than fifteen feet high that stood directly beneath the balcony of the great foyer, between the two staircases. "Are you ready for this?"

"Barely," she said, her eyes wide. "I'm already getting that bitten-off-more-than-I-can-chew feeling, so this should probably put me over the top. I mean—oh…my…*God*."

Once again, Sam felt himself looking through Paige's eyes as he gently pulled her along into the cavernous room. "Up there?" he said, pointing with his free hand. "That's the Balfour imitation of a minstrel gallery. Terrific for hiding out in and watching the dinner party going on down below, when everyone thinks you've gone to bed. Oh, and also unparalleled for launching paper airplanes."

"Paper airplanes? In here? That's just plain sacrilegious, Sam, shame on you. But I'll bet they sailed really well," Paige said, letting go of his hand and walking across the expanse, to the dining table. "How many does this seat? Forty?"

"Close. Forty-two."

She was lightly running her hands over the shining surface of the table. "And how many will make up this intimate dinner party?"

"Eight or nine. I'd like to set places for nine, in any case. How's that glass of wine sound to you about now?"

"Like a really, really good idea." She turned to look at him, those green eyes wide and faintly frightened. "It can't be done, Sam. Nobody could make this place feel intimate. Not unless we pitched some sort of fancy tent in one of the corners."

"A tent? You know, that idea might have possibilities. Which corner?"

Paige rolled her eyes at this remark. "I wasn't being serious, Sam. A tent would be…al-*though*…"

"I think I hear gears turning. Think out loud, Paige."

"I'm not thinking," she told him, beginning a circuit around the long table. "I'm musing. There's a difference. *But,* if I could sort of, you know, *disguise* this massive table with some sort of tablescape? It's so huge, maybe a couple, three, different tablescapes, you know? Then it would lose some of its overpowering *hugeness*. And not a tent, but…but a series of *canopies*."

"Canopies." Sam shook his head, trying to ignore the notion that she was too far away, when she was only standing at the opposite end of the table. "Nope, sorry. I don't get it."

"Yes, you do. Or you will. Canopies, Sam. Striped. Festive. The corners held up by what look to be long swords, or halberds, or whatever they're called—fancy axes with really long handles, okay? The material puddling on the floor, the tops all peaked and everything. A large-as-life English village, decked out for a Christmas Fair. Almost medieval, you know? These paneled walls, that high ceiling? Those *beams?* They just scream medieval."

Now Sam put a hand to one ear. "I don't hear any screaming."

"That's all right, Sam, you don't have to hear it. As long as I do. I can already *see* them, lined up against the walls. The tent, the one for the intimate dinner party, would fit right in, yet be it's own small world, and then the village itself would be perfect for the open house. Each canopy would be its own shop, its own stop in the buffet." She pointed at him. "Tell me the open house will include a buffet."

"I'd be afraid not to. So a buffet it is."

"Great! I know a caterer who'd be perfect. One of the stalls—they were called stalls, you know. Anyway, one of the stalls would be the carving station, for the Christmas joint of beef or whatever it's called. Two stalls set up as bars, one at each end of the room. Excuse me, each end of the *village*. Vendors dressed in medieval costumes wandering the crowd with trays piled high with pastries and things like that. Jugglers. Strolling minstrels. Wait! Not just strolling minstrels. Minstrels in the minstrel gallery, too. I mean, isn't that what a minstrel gallery is for?"

"So rumor has it, yes."

Sam was beginning to really like this idea. Lord knew the room was large enough to accommodate Paige's elaborate plans, measuring forty feet across and with a length of over seventy feet. He'd been in smaller houses. More importantly, Uncle Ned would like this idea. He might even like it enough to want to be a part of it. Uncle Ned and Maureen had thrown some damn good parties, years ago.

"So that's what we do. You can't just stick a table in here and say, hey, we're having a party. Not in a place this size. You've got to go big or stay home, right? Travel the whole nine yards, Sam. Please, Sam. *Please* tell me I can do this."

She looked so appealing as she walked toward him down the length of the table. He especially liked the way she was actually hugging herself now, her eyes shining like emeralds. You'd think he'd just given her the Hope Diamond, when what he'd really handed her was a damn whole lot of work.

"If you think you can handle it, all right. Go for it."

Her relief was obvious, as was her delight. "Oh, Sam, this is going to be *so* good. I can't believe how excited I am. Pink Christmas trees? Gilded hula hoops? From that—to *this?*"

"So this is where I get to say that I'm glad you're happy? Better yet, is this where you thank me?"

Paige dropped her arms to her sides for a moment and then walked straight toward him, to wrap those arms around his neck as she smiled up into his face. "Thank you, Sam. I mean it. Thank you so much. Right now I don't care why you're doing this, I simply *can't* care why you're doing this. Not when it's all going to be so great. You can't know what this means to me. Balfour Hall is like…like a magical playground. A fantasyland. The sort of thing I dreamed about as a little girl."

And then, as if she couldn't do anything else that would adequately show her thanks, she went up on tiptoe and kissed him on the mouth.

All right. He'd never thought of Balfour Hall as an aphrodisiac but what worked, worked.

Sam felt an immediate kick-start to his libido and began to slip his arms around Paige…just as she broke contact and pushed away from him, her eyes still shining.

"Come on, Sam, show me those photographs. You said you kept them in the library, right? Let me see if I can find it again without getting lost. And then tomorrow, I want to come back and see the decorations you told me about. Where are they?"

"Uh…in the storage rooms above the garages," Sam said, watching as Paige all but danced toward the doorway, eager to see the photographs he'd promised her, her high heels clicking against the wood floor, that ridiculously long scarf flying out around her and somehow accentuating her long, long legs. All golden blouse and beige slacks and scarlet scarf; again the slightly naughty Christmas angel.

She was so obviously genuine, so unconsciously beautiful. And so completely oblivious to the impact she'd just had on him with that impetuous kiss.

Well, damn. If he'd never thought of his family home as being an aphrodisiac, he'd never thought of Balfour Hall as competition, either….

Five

Paige accepted the snifter of blackberry brandy Sam had told her she'd enjoy more than another glass of wine, willing her hand not to shake. "Thanks."

Then she covertly watched him as he returned to the cleverly hidden small bar to pour a snifter of golden-looking brandy from another crystal decanter. He'd told her that blackberry brandy was too sweet for his taste, and more suited to hers, as she'd liked the wine he'd picked for her at dinner.

She'd answered him in nods and monosyllables, because she was still trying to figure out why the hell she'd hugged the man. Worse, she'd kissed him.

So much for that metaphorical chastity belt she'd strapped on with such conviction.

Not that the hug and kiss were all that bad. In theory. A gesture of thanks, that's all. In theory.

In practice? In practice, she was pretty sure that in another ten seconds she would have been prone on that baronial dining table, with her legs wrapped around the man's back.

Paige took a sip of the brandy. Sweet. Sort of thick in a way. Syrupy, even clingy. And, she hoped as she took another sip, medicinal. As in it might be a cure for transient stupidity.

She looked up from her seat on the leather couch as he walked toward her again, the snifter in one hand, a large photograph album tucked beneath his other arm.

"There are a dozen or more albums, but we can start with this one. It contains what my mother calls an overview of Balfour life, then and now. In other words, she got tired of trying to organize all of the thousands of photographs in chronological order."

"Are there any of you on a bearskin rug?" she asked him as he sat down beside her. "Or is that something parents don't torture their kids with anymore?"

"Torture?"

"Yes. You know. It's your first prom, and your mom pulls out the old photo album for your date, and turns straight to that picture of you bare-assed on a rug? It happens all the time on TV sitcoms."

"I guess I lucked out there," Sam said, putting his snifter down on the edge of the coffee table before laying the book down, too, and opening it. "But there is an empty space in here somewhere, because I ripped up the photograph—the only one in existence, by the way—of me smiling openmouthed at the camera with a mouth full of braces. Mostly, I frowned for about two years."

"Really? I'd wondered about that," Paige said, and then caught herself. "Uh, I mean, not the frowning, because you really don't frown, but how kids feel about braces. I didn't need them."

"You're lucky. I couldn't chew gum for two years, and that drove me crazy. What's strange is that I haven't chewed gum now for about twenty years, and I don't miss it."

"No, that's reasonable and very human. We often want most what we can't have," Paige said, and then inwardly kicked herself again. If the man commented on the weather, would she still be able to put her foot in her mouth with her response?

He captured her eyes with his own slightly mocking gaze. "And then, when we can have it, when we finally get it in our grasp, we don't want it anymore?"

"Okay. I suppose that also seems reasonable," Paige said, reaching for the top corner of the first page of the photograph album, and hopefully finding something she could use for a change of subject. "Oh, look, who is that? And would you take a look at that collar? You'd think he'd slice his ear off if he turned his head."

"I think that's called a celluloid collar," Sam told

her, his voice close to her ear. "That might be Samuel Edward Balfour II. Junior Balfour. Or else he's the third. Anyway, he's one of the numbered Sams. I should know this, shouldn't I?"

He'd touched a nerve, even if he couldn't know it. "Yes, Sam, you should. Family is important. Family is your heritage. Who they were helps make up who you are. This house, Sam? It's wonderful, it truly is a treasure to be proud of. But at the end of the day, it's family that really counts. Knowing your roots."

Then she shut up, because she was doing it again. Saying things she shouldn't say. They weren't swapping life stories here. The man was a client. Period.

"I suppose you're right," Sam said, reaching in front of her to turn another page. He kept turning pages, looking for photographs showing the house at Christmas. "My mother was into genealogy there for a while. I'll have to send these albums down to her so she can label some of these photographs. Okay, here's one. The great foyer."

Paige leaned forward, directing her gaze to the photograph Sam had indicated with his finger. What she saw was a little boy in a white shirt and short dark blue velvet pants, a bandage on his knee, smiling into the camera as he proudly held up a fishing pole with a big red bow on it. The little boy's eyes were *smiling*.

Something inside her chest went sort of spr-r-o-ing. *My, wasn't that sophisticated...*

"So, what do you think?"

Paige snapped back to reality a lucky heartbeat before she said, "About what?" She cleared her throat and said, "It's a good photograph, very inclusive. I think I can re-create that look. It's quite simple, actually, the live evergreen swags and bows and all. Old-fashioned, very traditional. I'll probably have to replace the bows, however. Those really don't hold up for too many years unless they've been stored very carefully. Who…um…is that you?"

"In all my glory, yes." Sam was still looking at the photograph, a small smile playing around the corners of his mouth. "I loved that fishing pole. I haven't thought of it in a long time, but I did love it." He turned to look at Paige. "There's a stream that runs through the property. Nothing but minnows and a few almost generic-types of fish too small to bother with in it, but that never stopped me from thinking I was going to reel in a whale. Mostly, I brought home frogs Mom wouldn't let me keep."

He wasn't trying to be charming, Paige was sure of that. Well, pretty sure of that. He simply *was* charming. Charming came naturally to him, like the air he breathed.

As battles of the sexes go, she had come into this one seriously underarmed and without a clear strategy. Time to back up a bit.

"A pony, your own stream to fish in—what else made up your childhood, Sam? Is there an indoor swimming pool or tennis court somewhere?"

He raised one eyebrow as he looked at her. "The tone is amused, but the question is a little pointed. What's going on here? I was doing pretty well there for a while. Did I just lose points because I had a happy childhood?"

"No, of course not. Don't be silly," Paige said, turning back to the photograph album. She hadn't meant to sound so sharp. "I had an imaginary friend when I was little. An imaginary sister, actually. Her name was Gretchen, and she was the brave one, the one who checked under the bed and in the closet every night, to make sure there were no monsters waiting to jump out and get me."

"Did she ever find any?"

Paige frowned as she looked up at him again. "Any what? Oh. Any monsters? No, she never did. But that didn't mean they weren't there. She just kept them away."

"Who keeps them away now that you're all grown up? Has Gretchen been replaced by a knight in shining armor? Should I be watching out for him and his great white stallion?"

This conversation was getting ridiculous, as well as increasingly uncomfortable. "I'm thirty years old, Sam, and hardly a child anymore. I slay my own dragons now."

"So no boyfriend," Sam continued. He was a very persistent man. "No one particular man in your life."

"No, Sam, no one particular man in my life," she

answered, tension bubbling along her nerves. "And, just in case you were going to ask, I'm not looking for one, either. My life is quite complete as it is. Now, either find me some photographs of the banquet hall or take me home, because this conversation is over."

"I thought we were talking too much, too," he said softly as he slipped one hand behind her neck and drew her closer. "Much, much too much talking…"

Paige could have resisted him. He wasn't holding her that tightly as he slipped his fingers into her hair.

But she was also intensely curious. Would Sam's kiss, in reality, be even remotely close to as devastating as she had already half decided it would be?

Besides, she rather liked the feeling of the shivery goose bumps his touch immediately raised on the back of her neck, an instant, pleasurable reaction that skittered down across her shoulder, a tingling that reached all the way to her fingertips.

Her lips parted, just a little, almost involuntarily, and she closed her eyes.

It had been a long time….

She lifted her arms to hold on to him as he eased her down onto the decorative cushions that were piled against the arm of the couch, their mouths clinging, his tongue initiating a sweet, welcome invasion she had no intention of denying.

His strong, hard thigh was between her legs, and she felt an instant tightening, a near burn of concentrated physical reaction of her most intimate being to the stimulus he provided, that the mere thought of what would come next provided.

Sam's moves were practiced, extraordinarily smooth, but Paige didn't care. She'd think about that later, think about all the other women who had succumbed to him at some other time.

Right now, it was her turn.

And it had been a very long time....

He had her blouse hem free of her slacks now, and she felt him expertly easing open the buttons of that blouse, one by one, as he kept his mouth fused to hers, his tongue working small miracles of arousal.

Her heart was pounding as he efficiently dealt with the front closing on her bra, freeing her breasts. He pressed the palm of his hand between them and held it there, as if to tell her that, yes, he could feel that frantic beat, too.

And that he liked the feeling.

Paige heard her soft moan of loss when his mouth left hers, but then arched her back as he turned his attention to her breasts, capturing first one nipple, then the other, leaving a trail of warm, moist kisses even as she felt the snap of her slacks release, even as her mind registered the soft sound of her zipper sliding open.

Oh, he was good. He was very, very good....

His mouth was next to her ear now. "Nobody wins, Paige, nobody loses."

"That's...that's not always true." She closed her eyes as the soft whisper of his voice seemed to send off small vibrations inside her ear, down the side of her neck.

"Are you planning to break my heart, Paige?"

She pushed gently at his shoulders, and he obligingly moved back so that she could look into his eyes. "I don't think that's possible."

"You'd be surprised at what's possible, Paige," he said, his gaze hot and dark and capable of curling her toes inside her shoes. "You feel it, don't you? You wouldn't be here if you didn't feel it. We both knew this was inevitable the first time we met."

Paige averted her eyes. "I…I don't know what you're—yes. *Yes,* all right? Inevitable."

He stroked the back of his hand down her cheek. "And that makes you angry? With me? Or with yourself?"

"With myself," Paige admitted quietly. "I know who you are, what you are. And yet…and yet, here I am."

"I'm not the bad guy, Paige. I'm a man, and a man who wants you. Very much. It's not just the sex, and that's not just a line. I think you could be…important to me. Necessary to me."

"You don't even know me."

"Correction, sweetheart. I've never known anyone quite like you. There's a difference. A difference I think we should explore."

Paige tried to summon a smile. "This is ridiculous. You're lying on top of me, I'm half dressed—"

"Half undressed. But I'm working on it."

"Don't interrupt. We're lying here, and we're having this deep, and deeply strange conversation. Part of me wants to continue that conversation, but the rest of me has totally different plans for the evening."

Sam's smile melted what was left of her resolve. "We can stop now, postpone that inevitability, or we can enjoy each other now. Just tell me what you want."

She raised her arms to press the palms of her hands against his cheeks as she lifted her hips suggestively. "I think…I think I want you to shut up and come here. If you're done talking, that is."

This time when he took her mouth she more than met him halfway. *In for a penny, in for a pound*— that was the old saying, wasn't it? He wanted her. She wanted him. As he'd said, some things were just inevitable.

When he put his hand between them to push down her slacks, she helped him by raising her hips. When he fumbled with his belt, she pushed his hand away and did the job for him.

All the while, their mouths were fused together, anticipating, simulating the act—his tongue thrusting, withdrawing, her mouth capturing, holding. Never had she felt such an intimacy of passion, this extraordinary *need*.

Paige was swallowed up by the soft cushions that insulated her from the weight of Sam's body as he made short work of protecting her, even that brief interruption bringing a moan to her lips.

And then he was inside her, filling her, and she wrapped her arms and legs around him in her effort to take all that he would give her.

Vaguely, as passion, want and sweet, escalating need replaced everything else, Paige wondered who at Holidays by Halliday was going to win the pool....

Sam made his way to the greenhouse that stood on its own some thirty yards away from the rear of the east wing of the house, checking the watch on his wrist and measuring the hour against rush hour traffic and the beginning of his meeting with several international bankers at the Balfour Building on Chestnut Street downtown.

But as he'd told Paige, you're gonna have to serve somebody, and Uncle Ned had called this meeting, named the time and place and Sam had no choice but to attend.

He opened the door to the greenhouse, closing it again quickly against the morning chill that had frosted the lawns of Balfour Hall, and called his uncle's name.

Uncle Ned lived for his flowers, and the greenhouse had been expanded several times over the years, until it now rivaled some of the local nurseries for size and capabilities. But what was money for, if it couldn't buy you a few toys?

Sam passed by a long table crowded with pots of a flower he suddenly recognized. It was tall, a little spiky, and with its flowers exactly like those he'd seen last night in the great foyer.

"Son of a gun," he said under his breath, feeling like a fool. Now he knew who put those fresh flowers in the great foyer once a week. Who put fresh flowers all over the house, for that matter. "I really have to slow down, start paying more attention to what the hell goes on around here.... *Uncle Ned?* Where are you?"

"Over here, Sam. Turn left at the table of amaryllis."

"I would, if I knew what the hell an amaryllis looked like! Keep talking, Uncle Ned, and I'll just follow your voice." Sam pulled the handkerchief from his back pocket and wiped at his forehead before shrugging out of his cashmere topcoat. You could roast an ox in this overheated building with no problem.

"Ah, see that you found me," Uncle Ned said, smiling. He was seated on a high stool, a rubber apron tied around his spreading waistline, the bib of the apron held in place by the loop of material slung around his neck. He had on bright green rubber gloves, and he was snipping at a sad-looking plant with a small pair of clippers. "Emergency surgery," he said, snipping off another small, limp branch.

"Really. Will the patient live?"

"It'll be touch and go for a while, but I think so, yes." Uncle Ned put down the clippers. "You didn't listen to me, Sam. I'm extremely disappointed in you. *Extremely* disappointed."

"I don't know what you're talking about," Sam

said, knowing damn full well what his uncle was talking about. *Whom* his uncle was talking about.

"Don't insult me. Paige Halliday isn't like your other women, Sam."

Sam nodded. He'd been thinking the same thing almost constantly since last night. The woman had gotten to him. How, he didn't know. He had already planned to see her again today, even if he had to make up a reason. "I agree. She's nothing like any woman I've known. That's her attraction. I'm allowed to be attracted, aren't I?"

"No, Sam, you aren't. I had Bruce investigate Ms. Halliday thoroughly before I chose her to receive one of my anonymous gifts. Did you bother to read Bruce's report?"

"Not really, no. Are you going to tell me what I missed? She's one of your do-gooders and a winner. She's also beautiful, desirable, unattached and—" Sam caught himself before he said, *willing*. "What else is there to know?"

Uncle Ned carefully eased himself off the stool and picked up the ailing plant, carrying it over to a table sparsely populated by other plants that looked like they'd seen happier days. "I shouldn't. You should care enough to read the report on your own. But I suppose you were too busy figuring out a way to…don't make me be crude."

"I wouldn't dare," Sam said, bending down to pick up a trowel he saw hidden half-beneath one of the tables. Uncle Ned was really upset. Why this sudden interest in his nephew's lifestyle? He'd never seemed to have any problem with it before. "What's going on here, Uncle Ned?"

Uncle Ned stripped off his rubber gloves. "I'm getting older, Sam. I'll be seventy-six on my next birthday. Your father, if he'd lived, would be seventy-two now. You'll be thirty-seven on your next birthday. Meaning, if you're counting, that your father was your age when you were born."

Sam only nodded. He nodded, because he had nothing to say. Uncle Ned was going to say it all. He knew his role for the morning, and it was that of listener.

"Maureen and I were never blessed with children, Sam. You were the only child born to carry on the Balfour name, the Balfour legacy, if you want to call it that, and sometimes, when I'm feeling particularly maudlin, that is what I want to call it. Before I die, I want to hold Samuel Edward Balfour VI in my arms. I want to see you happy, Sam, see you settled. You're the son I never had. Now I want a grandchild. I want to see the legacy."

"Grandchildren? You're talking about grandchildren? But there's plenty of time for all of that, Uncle Ned. After all, you're not going anywhere." Sam's deliberate smile faded as he waited for his uncle's answer, and his heart stuttered for a moment. "Are you? Uncle Ned?"

* * *

Okay, so she was an idiot. Perhaps even bordering on certifiable. What else could explain her behavior last night? After swearing to herself—hell, after swearing to *him*—that she wasn't going to get involved, wasn't going to become another of his transient love affairs, she'd folded like a house of cards as his laughing brown eyes had gone suddenly intense and mysterious.

And sexy. Sam Balfour had sexy down to an art form, no question. From his look, to his voice, to the way he smelled, to the way he slanted his mouth just so as he zeroed in for the kill. Oh, yeah. *Expertus-romanticus,* as the ancient Romans might or might not have said. He had it nailed, the whole routine.

"And then he nailed you," Paige heard herself say, and winced as her knuckles whitened from her tight grip on the steering wheel of the van. *Did you just hear yourself? One night with the guy and you're saying things like that? Thinking things like that?* She closed her eyes. *Already wondering when he'll drop you like a used car he's going to trade in for a new model but hoping he'll decide to get a few more miles out of you first? God, Halliday, you're pathetic.*

What was probably more pathetic was the way she was hunkered down in the driver's seat of the van that was parked out of sight behind a billboard just off the main highway, waiting for Sam's car to pass her on his way into the city.

He'd told her about a meeting he had downtown this morning when he'd dropped her off last night— after one last, long, searing kiss obviously meant to keep her thinking about him until she saw him again (and it had worked).

He'd also given her the code to the front security gates, obviously as a show of trust, which was nice, and told her to stop by any time to check on the decorations, measure staircases, whatever she needed to do.

It was all so smooth, so easy. She could slip into his life without a second thought, fall into his arms, his bed. He made it easy. He made it simple. No wonder none of his women saw the ax coming until it was too late.

Except they all knew the odds were that it was coming, Paige reminded herself as her stomach did a small flip at the sight of Sam's luxury car passing by on its way downtown. *You know it's coming—and he knows you know it's coming, because you have a big mouth, Paige Halliday, and you told him so. He has to figure that you know the rules and are okay with them.*

She put the van in gear and eased it toward the highway, now that the coast was clear. *When am I going to learn that I'm not as damn sophisticated as I'd like to think I am?*

Although Paige believed she had pulled it off pretty well with Mary Sue earlier, when her friend had demanded a minute-by-minute recap of the big date. By concentrating on describing the job, the sheer magnitude of the project, she had steered Mary Sue away from too many personal questions and then grabbed the digital camera and her favorite measuring tape. She'd escaped the office before Mary Sue stopped being giddy about how much money they were going to make on the job.

Now she was heading back to Balfour Hall, sneaking there like some thief in the night, avoiding the guy who had eased her back onto the soft cushions of an overstuffed couch and made love to her as if she was the most beautiful, desirable woman in the world.

Or at least for this week, she was.

And that's what Paige knew she had to remember every single moment she was in his presence. He was temporary, just like this job.

She stopped the van and leaned halfway out the window to punch in the code and then pulled the van through the opening and proceeded halfway up the drive before stopping once more to look at the imposing structure ahead of her.

Sam was right. The facade did put her in mind of Biltmore House, in its coloring, in the shape of its windows. But, large as Balfour Hall was, she could probably drop three of them into the Biltmore and have room for a five-car garage and a tennis court. So it wasn't *that* big. It wasn't ridiculously huge.

Yes, she could see it as somebody's home, although Sam must have rattled around in it a lot while he was growing up. A dozen children could have spent their days sliding down those banisters and playing hide-and-seek in the maze of rooms, and the place still wouldn't have been overcrowded.

That, she decided, was because of the design. The center block of the three-story building consisted of that immense foyer and its twin staircases in front of the banquet hall, which would soon house her miniature medieval village. Except on formal occasions, that center block was nothing more than a passageway from one wing of the house to its identical twin on the other side.

Sam said he lived in one wing, and as Paige drove around to the back of the house, she wondered which one it was. After all, they hadn't made it past the first floor, had they?

Now that she'd been *initiated,* would she make it to the second floor? And would she please, please stop thinking that she had somehow sold herself in exchange for a great job and some even greater sex?

Paige pulled the van next to the five-bay brick garages and checked her makeup in the rearview mirror before climbing out and going in search of Mrs. Clarkson, the housekeeper, to alert her that the designer would be poking around the premises.

Smoothing down the wool, three-button kelly green jacket she wore over a cream silk blouse and atop lightly pin-striped charcoal slacks—the ultimate professional look, she hoped—Paige was almost to the door Sam had told her she'd see directly across from the garages when the sun glinted off something in the far distance.

Curious, Paige turned away from the door and re-thought her idea of leaving her coat in the van. Then, since the sun was fairly warm, she shrugged and headed off across the grass, making her way around the large jut out of the banquet hall and toward the far wing. As she walked, she couldn't seem to stop turning her head left and right, to admire the enormous, curving terraces and the swimming pool that came complete with its own stone waterfall.

And, if she wasn't mistaken, there were two, no three, flags out there on the rolling grounds. Flags stuck on top of poles and the poles standing in the center of— Good Lord, the man had his own mini chip-and-putt golf course!

"Well, now, *that's* just obscene," she said, laughing.

The greenhouse she'd been steadily making her way toward, however, was not obscene. It was simply unbelievable. How could anything so modern, so huge, look as if it had been there since the house was built? The glass all looked old, the fittings aged copper and ornate, even as she heard the soft whir of modern machinery.

She was feeling the chill now and decided that it would be warmer inside the greenhouse. She'd just pop inside for a minute, and then she'd head back to see Mrs. Clarkson.

Well, at least it would sound like a good excuse if she was caught being so nosy.

Paige knocked on the door, doubting that knock would be heard above the sounds of a voice she recognized as Sarah Brightman's, singing her "Wishing You Were Somehow Here Again" solo from Phantom of the Opera, the lonely Christine lamenting the loss of her father.

That song, the poignancy of the words, Brightman's voice, always made Paige cry. There were a lot of people Paige wished could be somehow here again, most definitely her father and her mother.

She tried the door, and the latch depressed soundlessly, so she stepped inside, struck immediately by the heated, moist air, the heady scent of rich peat and what had to be more than one thousand flowers, and Brightman's voice climbing to a crescendo that threatened to shatter the glass panes above Paige's head.

"Hello? Is there anyone here? Hello!"

"'…help me say goodbye.'"

The glorious voice faded away, the music stopped and Paige heard someone call from deep inside the greenhouse. "I'm back here, two tables beyond and to the left of the amaryllis. Do *you* know what an amaryllis looks like, young lady?"

"I do, sir, yes," Paige said, making her way toward the strong male voice.

"Then you'll be a refreshing change from my last visitor," the not-quite-elderly man said, smiling at

Paige as she turned the corner to see him standing there, holding an empty clay pot in one hand and a trowel in the other. "And most definitely easier on the eyes. Hello, I'm Uncle Ned."

Paige's answering smile was quick and genuine. What a pleasant-faced man, from his shock of mussed silver hair to the smudges of rich black earth on his cheek. "And I'm Paige. Hello. Please excuse me for barging in on you like this. I was drawn in by the beauty of the building. And that marvelous music." Her smile widened. "And the flowers. You've got your own little heaven on earth here, Uncle Ned, don't you?"

"I do, yes. Just me, my music, my flower friends… and a few aphids, I'm afraid. But I'll vanquish them. I always do. You're the one who's going to deck the halls for Sam, aren't you? Big job. One could almost say too big a job for a pretty little girl like you."

"Are you flirting with me, Uncle Ned?" Paige asked as she leaned a hip against one of the sturdy metal tables.

"I could be," he said, winking. "But, at my age? How about I only offer you my flowers instead? I've got poinsettias back there, you know. All shapes and sizes. You'll be wanting the red ones."

"I'll be wanting lots and lots of red ones, Uncle Ned. How many do you have?"

"Enough. You'll need forty-seven of them to make up the tree. It has been some years, but I still keep those same plants going, year to year. It's all in knowing when to cut them back, when to hide them from the sun." He shrugged his shoulders. "And a little like the mother who still cooks for a small army, even when all the children are grown and gone, I suppose. It will be nice to put the poinsettias to work again."

"Sam said it's been a lot of years since Balfour Hall was decorated for the holidays. So that must mean you've worked here for a long time?"

Again, Uncle Ned smiled, and something about that smile told Paige she might have taken in the clay pot and the trowel and the smear of dirt and added them together to come up with the wrong impression. "You could say that, yes. I feel as if I've lived here for all my life. Is Sam paying you enough?"

The abrupt shift in conversation caught Paige unawares, and she only nodded. "More than enough some would say."

"He'll get his money's worth," Uncle Ned said, picking up the clay pot again and then looking at it as if he'd forgotten what he'd planned to put in it. "He always does…"

Paige looked at the man suspiciously. Were they having one conversation or two? There was a subtext there, maybe even a warning. She decided to test her theory. "Mr. Balfour's reputation precedes him, Uncle Ned. And I'm a big girl."

"And that was meant to tell me that you can take

care of yourself. Yes, I understand," Uncle Ned said, putting down the pot once more. "Let's go see those poinsettias."

Six

Sam had never in his life cut short a meeting for personal reasons, but he did that morning. It seemed only fair, as his mind wasn't on financial globalization but centered much closer to home.

His uncle had played his little game earlier and then watched to see how high Sam jumped before admitting that he was fine medically, just feeling old and lonely. But the exercise (that jumping to a worrying conclusion part) had set Sam's mind off in directions he didn't think it needed to take until he'd turned forty, at least. Wasn't forty the new thirty? He was just now entering his prime.

But Samuel Edward Balfour VI? Sam wasn't so

sure that Samuel Edward Balfour V was quite ready for that yet.

Although he probably shouldn't have said as much to Uncle Ned, who had immediately pointed out that then just maybe it was time Samuel Edward Balfour V "grows the hell up."

Marvelous.

Which brought Sam back to the subject, the person, who had been occupying his thoughts even more than his uncle's words—Paige Halliday. There was just something about that woman....

He'd screwed up last night, definitely. She'd pretty much thrown down the gauntlet, challenged him with her poor opinion of his lifestyle, and he'd used every trick in the book to break down her defenses, get her where he wanted her.

He couldn't complain that it hadn't worked. The dinner, Balfour Hall, giving her what she knew was a dream project, softening her up with endearing stories of his childhood. Luckily, he'd been a pretty cute kid. Talk about a good use of props; the photograph of himself and his fishing pole was one of his mother's favorites and would have melted the heart of a stone. And then, his timing perfect, he'd moved in for the kill.

What the hell was *wrong* with him?

Better questions: Why had he been so reluctant to take Paige home last night? Had he really thought about taking her upstairs to his bed, a bed no other woman had ever shared with him because he'd always kept his women separate from his private life? Why had he kissed her good-night and then walked away, only to turn back halfway down the walkway to go back and kiss her yet again?

When had he ever done that? When had he ever felt the need to do anything even remotely close to any of those things? When had he ever made love to a woman and then not automatically begin figuring out ways to get rid of her?

But she was different. Sam had told his uncle as much, and he meant it. There was just something more *real* about Paige Halliday. For one, she worked for a living. He couldn't say that about many of the other women he'd ever—

He'd ever *what?* Enjoyed? Used?

"Son of a bitch, I don't need this self-analyzing, navel-gazing crap," he grumbled to himself as he pulled the car around to the garages and saw Paige's van parked there. "I'll go in, I'll see her, I'll be pleasant because I'm stuck with her until Christmas Eve—something I should have thought about before I started this. But that's it. She's the wrong woman at the wrong time, showing up right as Uncle Ned starts messing with my head. There is absolutely nothing else going on here. Except that I'm talking to myself, and that can't be a good thing…"

Sam's resolve lasted until he ran Paige to ground in the banquet hall. He'd entered through the door to the second floor minstrel gallery, figuring he could stand up there, unobserved, and watch her as she worked. He'd have time then to really look at her, observe her as she was unaware of him, her guard down. She might not stir his blood today the way she had last night. Hell, since the first time he saw her with silver glitter turning her into a sexy angel.

He didn't know what watching her this way would prove, but it was the only idea he had, so he went with it.

But when he opened the door to the minstrel gallery, it was to see Paige standing at the curved railing, her back to him.

The woman definitely looked good from the back, her slacks curving enticingly over her buttocks and then dropping a long way toward the floor. She had great legs, and now that he knew what they really looked like, the slacks, no matter that they were gray and tailored, teased him with the fact that they were covering a true treasure.

The green jacket was all right, too, but Sam saw it as armor, hiding more treasures from view. A sweater would have been an improvement, losing the jacket. A soft fuzzy one, like the one she had on that first day.

Cripes. She was here on business. What did he expect her to wear, a satin gown that plunged to her waist front and back, a Come Hither sign pasted to her forehead?

Besides, the tailored gray slacks were just as successful as any satin gown.

So all right, so he could stick with Paige until Christmas Eve without considering it a sacrifice, a hardship. As long as they both—no, scratch that. As long as *she* knew their association would be temporary. *He* already knew that. Right?

Shaking his head slightly, because he was pretty sure some of the marbles inside it had come loose and needed a good rattle back to where they belonged, Sam quietly walked up behind Paige and bent to place a kiss on the side of her neck. "Found you at last," he said, whispered, into her ear. "Sometimes this house is just too big."

"Sam...hello," Paige said, keeping her back to him. "I, uh... Mrs. Clarkson told me you wouldn't be back until six."

Sam stood back, feeling rebuffed. Kissing her neck had felt good to him, but she didn't appear moved at all. "I know. I'm playing hooky. I figured you might need someone to hold the other end of the tape measure. What are you doing up here?"

"I, uh...just...nothing."

He stepped to the railing, looking toward her as she seemed to be sliding something inside her jacket. "What do you have there?"

"Nothing. Really. Just some notes I was... Oh, hell. All right, you caught me." She pulled the something from beneath her jacket and handed it to him.

Sam grinned, first at the paper airplane she was holding and then at Paige—who blushed very prettily. "Have another sheet of paper? You didn't fold this one quite right. You get more lift if you give it more wingspan."

"Really?" Paige turned to a tablet and pen he hadn't seen on one of the musician chairs and tore off another sheet. "Show me. I knew I was doing something wrong."

Sam looked over the railing and smiled again. There had to be a half dozen crashed paper airplanes littering the parquet floor of the banquet hall—and one more stuck in one of the quartet of large, antique crystal chandeliers.

Paige pointed vaguely out over the banquet hall as a whole. "That was actually looking like it would be my best effort, if the chandelier hadn't jumped into the way."

"Not nice to blame your failure on an inanimate object, Ms. Halliday. I can see you had a sadly deprived youth if you were never taught how to make paper airplanes. I, on the other hand, never make excuses. Of course, I am an expert in the area of paper airplane flying."

A shadow slid in and out of Paige's eyes almost too quickly for Sam to catch it. "Yeah, yeah, you talk a good story, Balfour," she said, handing him the paper. "Now let's see what you can do."

He took the sturdy page she handed him, glancing

down at the printing on it. Graph paper—a good weight for paper airplanes. "You use these to draw out your designs?"

"To scale, yes. I'm not that far with this project. I'm sorry to say that I'm still at the I-think-I-may-have-bitten-off-more-than-I-can-chew portion of the program."

"Which explains the paper airplane launch?" Sam asked as he deftly folded the paper.

"What can I say? I don't smoke and seldom drink. I have to have some sort of vice, don't I? Mine is wasting time doing things I shouldn't be doing when I'm not sure of what I should be doing."

Sam lifted one eyebrow as he smiled at her. "Would I be wrong if I thought *I* fell into that category? Something you shouldn't be doing?"

Paige screwed up her face at what he knew was a very bad joke. "Actually, you top the list. Now, show off your skills—not that you don't have skills in… I mean, show me what you can do. No! Scratch that. Just launch the damn airplane, all right?"

Sam's grin widened at her obvious frustration with herself. "You want me to go hunt up a shovel for you, or do you think you've dug deep enough all by yourself?"

"If I haven't disappeared yet, I'm not deep enough. I'm sorry, Sam. It's just… Well, I feel a little awkward. After last night…"

"All I've been able to do is think about you,"

Sam said as she lowered her eyes. "That's not a line, by the way, and honestly, all by itself, that doesn't make me happy."

Her head shot up. "Excuse me?"

Deciding he had a big mouth he'd be smart to keep closed for a while, Sam turned and launched the airplane. It dipped dangerously at first and then rose as it flew out over the banquet hall, making it to within ten feet of the other end of the expanse before landing almost gracefully on the parquet floor.

He rubbed his hands together in satisfaction. "I've still got it," he said teasingly.

"You've got something," Paige agreed. She made a circular motion with her hand, as if urging him to "spill it" if he had been about to confess to something. "You were saying…?"

"Nothing. I say nothing quite often. So, tell me about your plans for the big night. I've been giving some thought to the idea of roasting a pig in the fireplace, you know. But I doubt there's been a fire in there for over five years, so if you want roast pig, let me arrange to have the chimney checked out first."

"I already have that on the list. The cleaning, I mean, not the pig roast. I'd rather stick with a great hulking Yule log, if you don't mind. It seems traditional in a setting like this."

As she spoke, she tore off another sheet of paper and began folding it, mimicking the folds he'd made in his own paper. She was a quick learner…which maybe wasn't a good thing, not if she was dedicating herself to learning about *him*.

He put his hands over hers as she tried to make another fold. "No, not that much. Remember, you want to have lift. And how's your delivery motion?"

"Not as smooth and practiced as yours, that's for sure," Paige shot back at him, and once again they were in dangerous territory. It certainly didn't take much to get them there, either. Sam was getting the idea that they could begin a conversation about the weather and within moments be slinging double entendres back and forth about high pressure zones and prevailing winds.

"Touché." He stepped behind her and slid his left arm around her waist as he covered her right hand with his own. "All right, here's how you do it." He moved in closer, caught her subtle scent. "What's that perfume you're wearing? You smell good."

"Soap, I think," Paige said. He felt her taking in a deep, almost shuddering, breath.

"Only soap? Really?" If he could feel her pulse, he was pretty sure it would be racing. His ego, which frankly had been feeling a little bruised, took heart.

"Maybe my shampoo? I don't often wear perfume."

"You don't need it," Sam said quietly, slipping his right hand down over her wrist. "All right, here we go. Draw your arm back like this, hold nice and steady, don't forget to keep your preferred trajectory in mind as you bring your arm forward again, and—"

"What does that mean, exactly, when it comes to paper airplanes? Trajectory?"

"It means the same no matter how you use it. It's the path of a projectile or other moving body as it passes through space. In other words—never mind. Just launch it where you want it to go."

"Well, duh. That wasn't exactly helpful, Sam. I want it to go *out there,* of course. I'm not going to turn around at the last minute and throw it against the wall behind me."

Sam brushed his lips against the skin behind her ear. "If I'm going to teach you how to play golf, I can see I'm going to have to first stock up on patience and then maybe a couple of stiff drinks."

The words he'd just said replayed themselves in his head—golf? He'd just said he was going to teach her to play golf? Not in December, he wasn't. So did that mean he was thinking of Paige and at least several months into the future at the same time? What the *hell* was happening to him? Was this all Uncle Ned's fault, or hers? It couldn't be his. He was just an innocent bystander. Oh, all right. Not entirely innocent and not exactly a bystander. Not after the explosive passion of last night and certainly not after he couldn't get the memory of that passion out of his head today.

He let go of Paige's wrist and stepped away from her. "Why are women so prickly when a man tries to tell them something? Just toss the damn thing, all right?"

Paige kept her back to him. "Yes, sir. As you command, sir." Then she turned to look at him, paper airplane still held in her hand, poised for flight. "Are you trying to pick a fight with me, Sam?"

Sam was about to say *don't be ridiculous*. But maybe she was right. "I'm not sure. You?"

"It might be easier," she said, taking hold of the paper airplane with both hands, totally ruining the wings. "Oh, now look what I did! Go away, Sam. You make me nervous and stupid." She crumpled the airplane completely as she rolled her eyes. "Well, wasn't that a *sophisticated* thing to say?"

"It was an honest thing to say, and I think I'm flattered." He held out his hand to her, and she deposited the crushed airplane into it. "Not exactly what I had in mind," he said, smiling. "Come on, let's go down to the library and talk about your plans some more. I am your research source, remember."

"Not completely," Paige told him as she picked up her tablet and pen and followed him out into the hallway. "Uncle Ned has been very helpful. And he's so sweet. He guided me around the second floor of the garages, where all the decorations are stored, and showed me his poinsettias, which are absolutely gorgeous, and more than enough to give you a poinsettia tree that will knock your socks off."

Sam thought he kept his composure very well, considering that his mind was spinning in several directions. He knew he had to hear more. "Is that right?

Uncle Ned? *Sweet* Uncle Ned?" he asked, taking her hand and leading her toward the narrow staircase that led from the minstrel gallery to the ground floor.

"Your gardener, yes. I was looking around for— Okay, I was *snooping,* and saw that magnificent greenhouse and walked in. And found Uncle Ned. He likes you, you know. And I think it's wonderful that you keep him on, even though he certainly can't do heavy work around the grounds anymore. Then again, I'd say he's worth his weight in gold for the way he has with plants."

"Worth his weight in gold?" Sam hid a smile. That crafty old man! "Yes, I think we could safely say that. So, you met Uncle Ned. My gardener. What else have you been doing, besides getting paper airplanes stuck in chandeliers?"

He stood back to let her pass ahead of him into the Library, and then watched as her shoulders stiffened momentarily as she looked at the couch.

Thirty-five rooms in this place, and he had to pick the library. There was no question about it, he was losing his edge. And since Paige Halliday was the only new thing in his life—the only real complication in his life—he had only her, or himself, to blame.

She lifted her chin and turned to smile at him. "So? Did you find more photographs? I'd really like to know what was done with the crèche, where it was placed. It's gorgeous, and Uncle Ned told me each figure was completely hand carved in Spain. How you could have had it packed away above a garage for years is amazing to me."

"I know. I'm ashamed of myself. But you're going to correct all of that, remember?" Sam rubbed at the back of his neck, trying to concentrate on something other than the way sunlight was streaming in through the large oriel window and backlighting Paige in a way that made her seem outlined in gold.

"You haven't really given me enough time, but I'm going to try." She tipped her head to one side. "What are you doing?"

"Doing? Nothing."

"Yes, you are. You're looking at me that way again. Like I have a piece of spinach stuck between my front teeth, or like I'm an alien that just stepped out of its spaceship. Whatever you're doing—stop it."

"You don't want to be in this room, do you?" Sam asked her, as she hadn't moved since stopping a good ten feet away from the couch that was positioned in the middle of the library. "That's my fault."

Paige turned her back to him and walked around the couch, sitting herself down very deliberately and looking up at him in some defiance when he followed her. "You could *not* be more wrong. I'm perfectly comfortable in this room." She crossed her legs even as she spread her arms wide, relaxing back against the soft cushions. "See?"

He had to give her credit for guts.

He'd removed the photograph of Uncle Ned from

the album he'd shown her last night, and told her a photograph might be missing because he'd destroyed one of himself looking bad in braces. At the same time, he'd made sure she'd seen the adorable little kid with the bare knees and the brand-new fishing pole. Every move he'd made last night had been planned, cold and calculating, and like the district attorney always said in television drama courtroom scenes, *with malice aforethought.*

All in all, he'd played Paige like a fish he'd wanted to land with that new fishing pole. He was a shallow, manipulative bastard out for his own pleasure, through and through. That it had taken him nearly thirty-seven years to figure that out didn't make him any happier. Well, that thought didn't make him any happier right now, either.

"I seduced you, Paige," Sam said, feeling the rush of honesty flowing through his veins—or draining out of his head. Something was going on, he knew that much.

He pushed the photograph album to one side and sat down directly in front of her on the coffee table, looking levelly into her eyes. "Nothing about last night, nothing about anything that happened after we met in the coffee shop and you told me you knew me by reputation was spontaneous on my part. The offer to decorate this place, the intimate dinner, the house tour, the photograph of the cute little kid in the short pants, the whole nine yards. I planned it all,

Paige, and it all went down just the way I'd planned. And I'm sorry."

Paige didn't move. Her long legs remained crossed, her arms flung out casually along the back of the couch. Her gaze never left his; she never blinked.

The hands on the mantel clock paired up at the Roman numeral twelve. For the count of twelve, there was no sound in the room but the clear bell chimes of the clock striking out the hour.

Finally, Paige spoke.

"You must think I'm the lamest, most gullible female you ever met."

"No, no," Sam said quickly, leaning forward, his elbows on his knees. "I pulled out all the stops. After what you said to me? After what you told me about…about your college roommate…"

"Laura," Paige said, ice in her voice. "Her name at the time was Laura Reed."

Sam mentally winced, knowing he'd screwed up again. "Exactly. Laura Reed. I remember." Was Paige ever going to blink? He pinched at the bridge of his nose. "Where was I?"

"Digging your own hole this time. Let me help you out with that, all right? You were telling me you think I'm too stupid to know what we were doing last night—what *you* were doing last night, at least," she said calmly. "Have you ever done an IQ test on any of your dates, Sam? Because I'm guessing that my IQ wouldn't have to be much higher than that of tapioca pudding in order to beat out your usual play toy, Laura included. *Of course* I knew what you were doing. Now stop hovering like some penitent about to go down on his knees, and get out of my way. I want to stand up."

Sam was on his feet before everything Paige had said to him had fully registered in his brain. "Wait a minute," he said, taking hold of her arm as she tried to move past him. "I want to be clear on something here. Did I seduce you, or did you seduce me?"

Her smile landed a figurative punch to his gut. "Nice girls don't tell."

"No? Well, let me tell you something, Paige. You may look like an angel sometimes, but I don't think the nice girl defense is going to work here. Now. Are we having some kind of contest here, or is something else going on?"

For the first time, Paige looked apprehensive. "Contest? I…I don't know what you mean. We… we're both adults. We…enjoyed each other last night. You're the one trying to read more into it."

"Am I?" Sam reached up a hand and cupped the back of her neck. Tilted his head slightly as he brought his mouth close to her full, slightly parted lips. "This is all just…casual for you?" he asked her in a near whisper.

A small smile began to play around the corners of her mouth. "Let's just say I knew what I was doing."

He settled his free hand around her slim waist,

beneath her jacket. Their mouths were still only a whisper apart. "In that case, Miss Smarter-Than-Tapioca-Pudding…would you like to do it again? Only this time, you can pretend to seduce me."

And she was gone. Just like that, as he closed his eyes and moved in for the kill, he was holding air and probably looking like a major jackass.

"Not right now, thank you," she said from ten feet away, standing in front of the fireplace. "Tell me more about your father. You really do resemble him a lot."

Sam suddenly felt like a rank amateur. Smooth? He'd thought *he* was a player? Paige Halliday made him look as clumsy as a high school junior out on his first big date—with his second cousin, because his mom fixed him up after he couldn't get a prom date on his own. "Sure. What do you want to know?"

"Well…you told me he passed away some years ago and that your mother lives in Florida. Surely there's more."

"Uh-huh," Sam said, joining her in front of the fireplace, the two of them now looking up at the oil portrait of his parents. "Next question, *Why* do you want to know?"

"Idle curiosity?" Paige said, shrugging her shoulders. "Families…interest me. That's all."

"While kissing me doesn't."

"Not right now, no," Paige told him, amusement clearly in her tone, and then she actually patted his cheek. *Good dog. When we're done here, maybe you can have a little treat, all right?*

"My father was a teacher," Sam said, giving up. "Well, not exactly a teacher, not in the usual way. He was a world-class engineer, and he traveled overseas, teaching people how take care of themselves, drill wells, clean up their water supplies, avoid diseased food. He liked being an engineer, but he loved helping people, not just by writing a check, but by giving of himself. With as much Balfour family money as he had behind him, Dad could afford to love both what he was and what he did with what he was."

Paige stepped closer to Sam, actually leaned her head against his arm. "That's beautiful, Sam. Did you and your mother travel overseas with him?"

"Not me, no. Just my mother. Many of the places they went were considered too primitive and dangerous for a young child, and then I was in school and it was impossible for me to travel with them anyway. So I stayed here."

Paige lifted her head to look at him, her eyes wide. "By yourself in this huge house? With what, a nanny or something like that? Or did they ship you off to some boarding school? Oh, I'm sorry. You don't have to answer that."

"Why? I was fine. They were home for weeks at a time before they were gone again, and I wasn't exactly without people to watch over me until, yes,

I was old enough to go to boarding school. Which I liked, by the way."

He figured he might as well tell her everything. Sam took hold of Paige's hand and led her back to the couch, pulling her down with him but not letting go of her hand. "When Dad got sick, they came home. He had the best doctors, but he'd picked up some damn exotic bug somewhere, and by the time they'd figured out what it was, it was already too late. He couldn't beat it. And that's the story of my father."

"It's a sad story, Sam," Paige said, squeezing his hand, "and yet somehow beautiful. Clearly your father was very dedicated to what he was doing. You must have been devastated to lose him."

"Yes, I was," Sam said, looking across the room at the painting one more time. Maybe that's why he normally avoided this room. Because, as devastated as he'd been by the loss of his father, he'd been pretty damn mad at the man, too. Just as Sam had been coming into his own as a man, able to be on a level playing field with his father, the man was gone, and Sam's mother was as good as gone. They'd always been so complete in themselves, just the two of them, do-gooders on their lifelong mission—with Sam never really fitting into the mix very well.

But it had worked out. Uncle Ned and Aunt Maureen had in Sam what they couldn't have on their own. He'd been as much their son as he'd been to his own parents. Maybe more.

"Do you know something, Sam? I like you, and I have since I first met you. But I think I like you even better when you aren't trying so hard," Paige said, leaning in to kiss his cheek.

He laughed in a self-deprecating way and shook his head. "I've never had to work so hard before meeting you. My good looks, my natural charm—my money. They've always been enough. Mostly, the money. I'm not that vain, you know."

"You forgot to mention those sexy, smiling eyes or how modest you are with it all," Paige pointed out, smiling. "Ask me to go to dinner with you tonight."

He enjoyed seeing her smile. "All right. Will you, Ms. Halliday, do me the pleasure of joining me for dinner this evening?"

"Will squid be on the menu, Mr. Balfour?"

"Definitely not."

"I see. Will *you* be on the menu, Mr. Balfour?"

"I think that could be arranged."

Paige stood up before he could grab her and kiss her until her eyes rolled back in her head—because she was driving him crazy, and they both knew it.

"In that case, I'd be delighted. Now, if you'll excuse me, I have to get back to work…and figure out how to get a paper airplane down from a chandelier."

He remained on the couch, swiveling to watch her leave the room, her long legs doing something to his insides that probably wasn't a good thing this early in the day. "And no tapioca pudding for dessert!" he called after her and then smiled as he heard her clear laugh from the hallway.

He spent five minutes looking at the portrait of his parents and then went upstairs to find the green folder with Paige's name on it....

Seven

Anxious to get away from Balfour Hall and its owner, Paige drove back to Holidays by Halliday pretty much on autopilot.

If she'd had anything to drink, she'd have to say she was drunk. What else could explain how she behaved whenever Sam was within ten feet of her? When he was within five feet of her, she turned into someone she barely recognized. When he was closer than that, the sensible, reasonably intelligent, modest, normally morally upright and at least marginally uptight Paige Halliday disappeared completely.

She had to get a grip here, remember who she was and who he was.

Maybe after tonight…

Paige blew in through the front door of her shop, her mind still anywhere but on business, to see Mary Sue wrestling with an enormous garland that seemed to be getting the best of her.

"Here, let me help you," she said, picking up one end of the garland that was constructed of fake greenery and decorated with pretty red cardinals and golden Christmas balls. "What's this for, anyway?"

"Well, damn," Mary Sue said, hefting the garland onto a worktable. "Here I was hoping you knew the answer to that one. I couldn't find an order form anywhere in the box. All I know is it came from Claire and the box was marked Rush."

Paige frowned. "Oh, wait, I remember now. This is the staircase drape for the Henderson house. Remember, Mary Sue? First it was white doves, but then some helpful pain in the neck told her white doves in a house were bad luck, or something. Her big party for her husband's employees is this Saturday night, so thank God this arrived, or I was going to have to go hunt up three dozen red cardinals and replace each dove by hand in the first garland. Is anyone free to take it over there to switch the garlands out, or do you want me to do it? Because I can do it. Trixie Henderson could talk the ear off a donkey, and she'd drive you crazy."

"No, that's all right, Paul can handle it, and he could probably talk the other ear off the donkey, so he and Mrs. Henderson should cancel each other out," Mary Sue said, the garland finally wrestled back into the carton. "How's it going at the mansion? We've been having a real ball here, I have to tell you."

Paige headed for the back room and the coffeepot. Mary Sue made great coffee, and Paige had decided she needed to *sober up* before she saw Sam again. "Do you have to tell me? Or would I be happier in my ignorance?"

"Oh, no, you're not getting away that easy. If I have to suffer, you have to suffer. I got a call at home at three o'clock this morning, since I'm your alternate emergency number and you, it would seem, were unavailable. I take it last night was a success— for somebody."

Paige turned back to the coffeemaker, pretending to top off her cup. She knew exactly where she had been at three o'clock this morning, who she'd been with and what had been happening at that time. "Three o'clock? Really? I must have slept through the phone ringing. I'm really sorry, Mary Sue. What sort of emergency? This building's still standing, so obviously not a fire. Although," she added, looking around the room and the controlled chaos it contained, "it might be hard to figure out whether or not we've been robbed."

"Very funny, but if you want to see chaos, come to my house. I'll be ready for Christmas, oh, around next February. Anyway, nothing happened here,"

Mary Sue told her, motioning for Paige to move so that she could pour herself a cup of coffee. "The mall, however? That's a whole other story. You do remember the Twelve Days of Christmas tableau-type thing we set up, right?"

"Right," Paige said warily. "Is this going to be like the turkey thing? Something fell over and hurt somebody? At three o'clock in the morning?"

"No, not quite, but thank you for playing our game. Unless you'd want to give it another shot—no, don't. You'd never guess, and let me tell you, the night watchmen or security guards or whatever they call themselves have some big 'splaining to do. As in, where the hell were they?"

Paige headed for a worktable and one of the stools. "Oh, boy, what happened?"

Mary Sue grinned. "Remember the eight maids-a-milking mannequins, Paige? They were still milking, all right, but not the cows. Let's just say the ten lords a-leaping—having somehow lost their pantaloons—were all wearing big smiles on their faces, okay? Making two of the maids ambidextrous, in case you're wondering about the math, or just overachievers. Our only good luck was that the mannequins aren't ana-tomically correct—but anyone with half an imagi-nation could easily fill in the, well, the missing parts."

Paige got a sudden mental picture she was sure would be burned into her retinas for a long time. "Oh, God…"

"Yeah. You're getting the idea, I guess? There were other bits of rearranging—weird crossbreeding going on with the geese and the hens and swans—although I probably don't have to spell that all out for you more than that. I will say that two of the piping pipers definitely would get a double-X rating. But, relax, it's all fixed now, finished before the mall opened for the early-bird walkers. I'm thinking college prank or fraternity initiation, or something like that. This was all a little too well done for high school kids."

"I should have been there," Paige said, guilt flushing her body. "I shouldn't have taken the job Sam offered, no matter how terrific it could be for us. We were already too busy."

"Oh, right—about the Balfour job?"

Paige closed her eyes for a moment. "Is this more bad news?"

"That depends on your idea of bad news. Your timetable—I looked at it—has you completing that job by the twenty-third, in time for this Christmas Eve party our handsome client is giving, right?"

"Right," Paige confirmed carefully. "I hadn't seen the place yet so I was flying by the seat of my pants when I wrote up that schedule yesterday afternoon. I built in a couple of extra days, but that's my target. Ten days, probably working Sundays, too."

"Well, don't look now, but the target just moved. I would have told you right away, but I figured the

Twelve Days of Christmas thing would relax you, make you laugh, before you went into panic mode."

"And here you thought you knew me so well," Paige quipped, rolling her eyes.

"Sorry about that. I agree, I shouldn't have waited. I got a call two hours ago from our favorite Philadelphia newspaper. They want to do a full-color spread on Balfour Hall in the Style section on the twenty-first. Complete with an interview with the designer, which is the icing on the cake. That call ended when Channel Six beeped in, and they've now got us for a video segment on the same day. Twenty minutes ago I got another call, this one from—*ta-da!*" Mary Sue held up a copy of the most important women's magazine in the country. Not just Philadelphia or the Tri-State Area—the entire *country*.

Paige felt her eyes nearly popping out of her head. "Don't play with me, Mary Sue. That's not funny."

"Do you see me laughing here? I'm already planning exactly when I should ask you for a huge raise, because we're taking off now, Paige, straight into the big time. They'll wait until the twenty-third, since their article won't come out until next October, in time for next Christmas. They plan ahead, you understand. I got all the dope from my new friend Mandy, the managing editor."

Paige sat very still for a full minute, her mind racing, and then got to her feet. "Get me a complete rundown of the projects we've still got on the burner—there can't be that much left to do on any of them, public or private—and a guesstimate of how much maintenance you think any of them will need between now and Christmas. Watering the live plants and making sure nothing fell over, nothing blew away, nothing got ruined by the weather, that somebody's dog hasn't chewed on it or that somebody's kid hasn't popped all the glass balls with a baseball bat—that sort of thing. The usual. Check last year's records. They'll give you a good idea."

"Wait a minute. Slow down," Mary Sue ordered, grabbing a pen and a notepad and scribbling furiously for a few moments. "Wait until I tell my kid that he's having Christmas in late February this year. Okay, ready, fire away."

"Get me another list of how many people we have, how many more we'll need. I'm hoping none. Get Sally Burkhart on the phone—you know, from the design school. I'm betting she'll loan me some of her students since they'll be going out on Christmas break soon anyway. I want a full team of strong backs assembled and waiting for me outside the gates of Balfour Hall at seven o'clock tomorrow morning, and tell them to bring bag lunches, because we're going to be there all day. There's two mountains of stuff in the rooms over the garages, and it all has to be brought to the house, unpacked, sorted, cleaned up and put where it belongs as soon as I know where it all belongs. And greens! Order greens, and have them delivered straight to Balfour Hall."

"How many greens? Can you give me a ballpark figure?"

Paige pictured the mantels, the double staircase in the great foyer. "Call somebody and take whatever they've got in stock, all of it. Only then can we start on the village in the banquet hall. Oh—I need a Yule log. Think giant redwood, and then go just a little bit smaller. And then find someone else to man the phones here, because you're coming with me. I can't do this without you."

Mary Sue grinned as she made a snappy salute. "Yes, fearless leader. I hear and I obey. I knew you'd come through on this. Oh—and I just decided that *now* would be the perfect time to ask for that raise."

An hour before Paige was scheduled to show up at Balfour Hall, Sam went in search of his uncle, who had done a pretty good job of avoiding him all afternoon.

He found him in the library, one of the photograph albums open across his knees. "Hello, Sam. I've found a good number of photographs that should prove helpful to Ms. Halliday. They're already stacked up on the desk over there."

"Good for you. Good for her. Why didn't you tell me?" Sam asked, walking over to the desk and leaning against it as Uncle Ned sat at his ease on one of the wingback chairs.

"I don't know, Sam. Why didn't I tell you *what?* There's such a multitude of subjects to choose from, you know."

Sam rubbed at his forehead; his headache had been on its way out until he realized his uncle was going to make him do a verbal dance before he told him anything.

"I read her file."

"Did you now?" Uncle Ned said, closing the photograph album. "A little tardy, but better late than never, I suppose. Is this going to be a general discussion, or is there something specific in Ms. Halliday's file you'd like to highlight for me?"

"You may look like the proverbial jolly old man, Uncle Ned, but at the bottom of it you're a real piece of work. You picked her on purpose, didn't you?"

"On purpose? In what way, for what reason? Go on. I'm certain you have formulated an interesting theory. Why don't you expand on it so I understand where you're coming from?"

Sam set his jaw for a moment, and then gave it up. You didn't win with Uncle Ned, nobody did, not in his heyday and not now. The most you could hope for was to break even. "Bruce is very meticulous, Uncle. He puts a date on everything. That file originated nearly two years ago, and it's been regularly updated ever since."

"I'm also very meticulous," Uncle Ned suggested, smiling at Sam.

"I would have said devious. Then I checked the other files from this year's crop of do-gooders. Those files were started this year and ran for no more than a month before you had me send off the gifts, the money, whatever."

"I see nothing untoward in that. Sometimes it takes longer for me to make up my mind about a subject. Pour yourself a drink, Sam, and sit down. Tell me what's bothering you."

Deciding that might not be such a bad idea, Sam poured himself two fingers of Scotch and returned to lean against the front of the desk. "You picked her."

"You're repeating yourself now."

"You picked her—*for me*."

Uncle Ned's smile grew slowly. "Oh, very good, Sam. Frankly, I was beginning to worry about your powers of deduction."

Sam pointed his glass at the man. "Thank you, you old conniver, but I'm not done. There's more. She's local, so you could have Bruce keep pretty close tabs on her until you were satisfied with your choice. And, because she's close, it even made it semilogical for me to take Bruce's place and deliver the letter."

"Getting the two of you face-to-face, yes. I worried that it might be too obvious, but you didn't catch on, did you? I think you were too angry with me for saddling you with my project—which you loathe—and too captivated by my Ms. Halliday."

"*Your* Ms. Halliday. You admit it." Sam shook his

head. "God. How could I be so stupid? You've been leading both of us around on leashes, haven't you?"

"Not really, Sam. I only found her and then also devised a way to put you two together. Anything after that was—and remains—a bit of a crapshoot. You do realize that the problem I had to wrestle with was that, in the normal course of your social life and your incessant womanizing, your paths never would have crossed."

"What would you have done if I'd just met her, handed her the letter, and walked away?"

"You did, Sam, at least for a few days. I'll admit that I was about to fall back on my Plan B and hire Ms. Halliday to decorate Balfour Hall, when you finally gave in and went after her on your own. Also having the annual dinner party here was your invention and probably looks now like at least a small payback for my intervention. Please consider me duly chastened."

"You're not even close to *chastened*."

"True. I'm fairly happy, as a matter of fact, especially after meeting Ms. Halliday, speaking with her. She's delightful."

"And nearly as complex as you, although you probably won't believe that," Sam interrupted, remembering his and Paige's earlier sparring match. "She might even be smarter than I am in a few ways."

"Is that so? Good, then she's even a better match for you. I won't even point out that, while I was—to be blunt—*playing* you, you were happily believing that you were playing *me*. Using my project to get to Ms. Halliday and at the same time slip in the bonus of forcing me out of my doldrums? What a coup it must have seemed to you. Neither of us is free of sin in this, Sam. You're definitely my nephew."

Sam looked at his uncle through narrowed eyelids. "I just thought of something else. Where's Bruce?"

"Bruce? After bringing me the photograph of you standing in an alleyway, covered in imitation snow, you mean? In Hawaii. His…let's say his flight was unexpectedly delayed a few days."

"Until I came to my senses and went after Paige and ended up executing your Plan B for you. But you fought me on the idea of decorating this place, having the dinner party here. You might have even looked frightened about the prospect."

"Yes. I'm good, aren't I? You're also good, Sam. You run our companies very well. But I still have some moves left that you haven't seen before."

Sam drained his glass. "Like letting me think you might be ill."

"That was pretty low, and I apologize. But I woke you up, didn't I? Life moves on, whether you want it to or not. Someday I won't be here, Sam. I love you, and I want you settled in time for me to enjoy seeing your happiness."

"And Samuel Edward Balfour VI," Sam said quietly. "You really spooked me with that one. And you're obviously serious, or you wouldn't have decided to open up Balfour Hall after all these years."

"I can listen, Sam, as well as give out advice. It is time. Maureen would be angry to know I've dug myself in here so deeply that I'm afraid to come out again. She might even have called me a coward, as she was the bravest woman I've ever known. Paige Halliday is right for us both, Sam, in many ways. And you do like her, don't you?"

Sam looked up at the portrait of his parents. "She gave the van to an orphanage. Lark Summit."

"Yes, we've established that," Uncle Ned said quietly, as if he knew they were now treading dangerous waters.

"I saw the newspaper clipping about the little girl at the orphanage who's undergoing chemo. Paige's hair is as short as it is because she donated her hair two months ago, to have a wig made for the child."

"Leaving little or no question as to her fine heart, her dedication or her character, I know. Did you read the entire file?"

Sam studied the bottom of his empty glass, as uncomfortable now as he had been when he read the file. "She grew up at Lark Summit. Parents unknown, never adopted, only two tries at foster parents that didn't work out. She…ah…she asks a lot of questions about family. She has told me that family is very important. And I laughed her off, even said something asinine about her having a deprived childhood because she didn't know how to fly a paper airplane. She never let on how that comment must have hurt her. She never said a word about her gift, what she did with it."

He lifted his head and looked at his uncle. "I'm a real ass here, Uncle Ned. I'm not looking good here at all, not to me, not to her, not to anybody. I tried to treat her the way I treat other women."

"Interchangeable. Dispensable. Convenient."

Sam held up one hand, smiling wryly. "That's enough. Nice of you to keep a list, but yes, you're right. So my question is—why did you subject Paige to me, since I'm such a bad ass?"

"Timing is everything, Sam, in business, in life. When I first learned about Ms. Halliday and her devotion to Lark Summit, you weren't ready for someone like her in your life. But I've sensed a restlessness in you this past year, even the slowly dawning realization that your life isn't as perfect as you'd like to believe it is, as it seemed to you when you were in your twenties, your early thirties. As long as we're being truthful here, I was holding the young lady in reserve, until I thought you were ready."

"Funny, I never noticed the strings," Sam said. "But that doesn't mean I'm not your puppet."

"You're angry," Uncle Ned said, getting to his feet. "You have every right to be, son, and I'd be sorry if I didn't think I've done the right thing. You're seeing Ms. Halliday again this evening? And, according to Mrs. Clarkson, she's coming here? That's a first for you, Sam, what with your belief that a smart bird doesn't—well, we both know the rest of that statement."

Sam nodded. He really didn't trust himself to speak, not just yet. Anger might make him say something they'd both regret.

"Good. Now here's a bit of either timely or unfortunate news for you. Tomorrow morning I need you to leave for Singapore. You should be back in time for the party, if you work very hard."

Sam's head shot up. "Singapore? There's nothing going on in Singapore."

"Don't say that until you check the folder I had Mrs. Clarkson put on your desk upstairs. Chang Industries has unexpectedly come on the block, or it will, in three days. I want you there, I want the inside track before the general announcement. Better yet, get our offer in before anyone else even knows the company is for sale. We've wanted Chang for a long time, Sam, and now's our chance. We could find someone else to go in your place—it would take three of our people to replace you—but I think a little distance between you and Ms. Halliday might not be a bad idea at the moment. After all, she's going to be very busy for the next two weeks. But I'll be here, to watch over her."

"Right, that's another thing. She thinks you're one of the gardeners."

His uncle suddenly looked ten years younger, his smile wide, his eyes nearly dancing in his head. "Our Ms. Halliday is in for more than one surprise on Christmas Eve, isn't she, Sam? I find that I'm quite looking forward to the evening." Then he sobered. "Try not to screw this up, Sam. You've got tonight and then two weeks to think about what's been holding you back from finding real happiness. I've every confidence you'll know what you need to do to secure that happiness after being on your own to think about it all."

"Absence makes the heart grow fonder?"

Uncle Ned shrugged. "There's another one. Out of sight, out of mind. No matter what happens or doesn't happen between you and Ms. Halliday, I think you might finally begin to understand what makes Sam Balfour tick."

"With the women I—let's just say I know who they are, what they are. I'm up front with them, and I know what they're about, what they're after. Men or women, in business or socially. I just don't like— no, scratch that. I'm not comfortable around do-gooders. I don't—present company excepted, of course—I don't trust them."

"Yes, son, I know. Did you ever ask yourself why?"

Paige held up two bags when Sam met her at the side door of Balfour Hall at six-thirty. She put a bright smile on her face, trying to ignore the small flip of her stomach as he stood in front of her, dressed casually in navy slacks and a soft knit shirt open at the neck. "I didn't know if you were a Geno's Steaks person or a Pat's King of Steaks person. Since they're right across the street from each other, I picked up cheesesteaks from both places, and you can pick your favorite. Is that all right?"

"Sounds and smells good to me," Sam said, standing back to let her come in to what turned out to be a very nice foyer, certainly smaller than the great foyer, but impressive anyway. "Let's go upstairs. I asked Mrs. Clarkson to set out napkins and an assortment of drinks for us."

Paige nodded, suddenly at a loss for words. Once she went up those stairs, the conclusion of their evening was pretty much a given, and they both knew it. "It might be less messy if we ate in the kitchen?" she suggested, hesitating.

Sam took the bags from her tight grip as he leaned in to lightly kiss her cheek, and kept his mouth close to her skin. "You don't want to come upstairs to see my etchings, little girl?"

"Very funny," Paige shot back at him and headed for the staircase. She was halfway up the flight before she realized the score was already Sam, one, Paige, zip. Not that she was keeping score, but it probably wasn't a bad idea to at least remain alert.

She stopped at the top of the stairs and looked around at a second small foyer, splendidly decorated in deep, rich woods and antiques. She tried to get her bearings and then headed through the open archway into what looked to be a living room. A very large living room, comfortable and welcoming.

Sam was right behind her. "Keep going. Dining room is on your left, through those double doors."

"This is nice," she said as she joined him at a dining table that probably could seat twelve at the most. "A real family dining room. Not at all like the banquet hall."

"Right. It doesn't have an echo," Sam said as he dumped the bags, one after the other, onto a bone china platter. "God, these really do smell good. Cheesesteaks are all ours, you know, just as much as Ben Franklin and hot pretzels and Rocky Balboa. Often imitated, never duplicated. If you ever see the words *Philly cheesesteak* on a menu anywhere else in the world, don't fall for it. Nothing comes close."

Paige began to relax. He was Sam, no matter that they were sitting here in his mansion, no matter that he was going to be no more than a temporary blip in the radar of her life in a few days or weeks, no matter that she thought they should have a chance for so much more. There was always time for regrets. For now, she'd live in the moment.

"You should do TV ads. Except who would you do them for, Geno's or Pat's?"

"I'd have to stand in the middle of Passyunk Avenue and just point in both directions, I guess." He grabbed a steak in a Geno's wrapper and put it on his plate. "Your turn."

"It only seems fair that I take a Pat's," Paige said, reaching for another wrapped steak sandwich. Then she got to her feet. "You said there were drinks. Let me get you something."

His mouth full, Sam pointed toward the far corner and the bar setup there, and Paige grabbed them each a longneck bottle of beer out of a silver bucket crowded with ice. Beer, in a silver champagne bucket. It was true: the rich *were* different.

As they ate, Sam gave her more information about the house, how it had always been decorated for the holidays, and promised her more photographs before she went home. She told him about the phone calls from the media and thanked him for arranging the publicity. He said it was the least he could do and reached for a second cheesesteak, this time a Pat's.

She caught him looking at her a little bit strangely a couple of times, but then thought she was overreacting, reading things into his glances that just weren't there. In her turn, she had to remind herself to stop looking at him as if he was on the dessert menu.

When Paige couldn't eat another bite, she pushed back from the table and put her hands to her stomach. "I probably shouldn't say this, but I think I liked tonight's dinner even better than last night's, in the restaurant. You can't eat with your hands in restaurants."

"You like to do things with your hands?" Sam asked,

winking at her before downing the last of his beer, and they were immediately back in "uh-oh" territory.

"I run a design business. Very hands-on. So, yes, I suppose so," she said, deliberately playing dumb. Then she smiled. "I like touching things…tactile, you know? The different textures, the varying shapes, and how to best combine them, make them fit together in satisfying ways. I love the softness of goose down, the deep caress of velvet, the coolness of silk slipping through my fingers, the almost sensual warmth of fur."

She thought that would do it…and she was right. After all, they were adults—consenting adults. They both knew where this was heading, so why not cut to the chase?

Sam held out his hand to her, and she took it, allowing him to draw her to her feet and out of the dining room, back into the living room. He stopped in the middle of the room and turned to face her. "So that's your favorite of the senses?" he asked her, putting his hand to her cheek, lightly stroking her skin with his knuckles. "Touch?"

"It…it, uh, seems a good place to start, yes," Paige said, knowing that from here on out it was probably best if she didn't think too much. "You?"

"I'm a fan, yes," Sam said, moving his face close to her ear. "Smell is also all right. Like, you smell really good, Paige." He drew back and smiled. "A whole new advertising strategy for Pat's and Geno's. *Eau de cheesesteak.* It could be a big seller."

Behind them, a fire blazed in the fireplace, but Paige was pretty sure that wasn't why she felt so warm. "I was going to mention the sense of hearing, but I think the cheesesteak perfume as a turn-on line sort of lost me. How about moving right on to taste?" She went up on tiptoe and pressed her open mouth against his, their tongues instantly dueling as his arms went around her, as her hands sought out the strong planes of his chest.

Her eyelids fluttered closed as he lifted her into his arms while still kissing her and walked with her back to the foyer and beyond.

Sensations both familiar and alien delighted and frightened Paige as she felt herself being lowered onto an already turned-down bed, Sam leaving her only long enough to kick off his shoes and remove hers…kissing the arches of her feet before moving up on the mattress, to end with his forearms braced on either side of her head.

He smiled down at her, although, just this one time, that smile didn't seem to reach his eyes, which remained deadly serious. "Number five, Paige. Sight. I knew you'd look good here," he said quietly. "I've been imagining you here for most of my life. I just didn't know it."

She wanted to believe him, longed to believe him. Maybe even needed to believe him.

"I don't know what's happening here, Sam," she said, perhaps revealing more of herself to him than she should. As she'd told him before, she knew who he was, what he was. She'd heard the stories, read a few of them on the Internet. Seen the photographs of all the beautiful women he dated. "I thought I did, but I don't. I mean, I talk a good story but—"

"Shh," he whispered, his fingers busy unbuttoning her blouse. "If we're starting over, you're going out of turn. Talking—hearing—was third. Touch comes first." His hand closed around her breast, the heat of his palm radiating down, down, setting off an answering warmth deep between her legs. "Touch me, Paige…"

Her heart pounding, her breaths becoming shallow and quick, Paige welcomed his invasive kiss as she tugged at his shirt, pulling it free of his slacks before pressing her hands against his bare back.

His skin was on fire, fevered. Like hers.

He shifted slightly, brought his mouth to her breast, captured her nipple through the sheerness of her silk bra, and she was able to slide her hands forward, undo his slacks and push them out of her way.

Touch. He wanted touch.

She wanted touch.

Touch…and taste.

And the sweet sound of his sigh, more nearly a groan, when she found him, grasped him in her hand. Warmth, heat, silkiness, softness, strength. Velvet over steel.

Sam put his arm beneath her back and pulled her

up with him so that they were sitting closely together, facing each other on the bed. His brown eyes had gone dark as night, and she watched him watching her as he slid her blouse from her shoulders, rid her of her bra.

She saw a quick flicker in his eyes as he reached for the front opening of her slacks and helped him push them and her panties down over her knees and beyond. He was so intent on what he was doing, and he did it so well.

That part she would forget about, his obvious expertise. She only wanted to know what he was doing to her, now. He was undressing her with his hands, yes. But it was more than that. He was undressing her with his eyes, with the way he touched her, as if worshiping every new revealed inch of her.

He drew her lower against the small, supporting mountain of pillows and now his mouth followed the trail his hands had blazed, kissing the hollow between her breasts, lightly tonguing her sensitive navel, skimming the tip of his tongue across her lower belly. The sensitive flesh between her thighs tightened and released, her every nerve ending tingling.

In anticipation.

He eased her legs apart and moved lower, slipping one of the pillows beneath her buttocks as he raised her up even as she bent her knees and braced her feet against the mattress, opening herself to him. There was no modesty, no shame. There couldn't be, not when Sam kept looking at her that way, as if filled with wonder.

Paige felt tears pricking behind her own eyes, so awed by the worship in his, and then let her eyelids flutter closed as he joined her in the most intimate kiss lovers could exchange.

His mouth was hot and moist against her, his tongue magical as he explored, flicked, lightly suckled. He used his fingers to spread her, invade her, and followed each foray into new territory with his warm breath, his curious tongue. Paige gritted her teeth as he took her high, then higher, sending showers of delight through her that she'd never known were possible.

And then the urgency took over, a *want* so elemental, so strong, that she gave up dominion over her body and ceded all power to him. His fingers, his mouth, were doing things to her that sent her flying so high she forgot to breathe, could not breathe. All she could do was cling to the ecstasy he brought her, until the effort became too much and she let go, her body pulsing and clenching, racked with pleasure.

"Sam!" She reached out blindly, begging him to come to her, to hold her, to let her hold him as she tried once more to anchor herself to reality.

But then a new sensation overcame her, and she knew she wanted to give. She had taken, and the taking had been wonderful. But it wasn't enough.

"Sam…?" Paige swallowed hard on the tight knot

of tension and passion rising in her throat. She wanted him, every bit of him. She wanted to crawl inside him, become a part of him. She dared again to reach her hand down, to touch him intimately. "Sam. Let me…"

He looked at her, looked deeply into her eyes, his own naked and vulnerable. And something else. Something she couldn't put a name to, was afraid to attempt to identify—because if she was wrong, her heart just might break.

"Please," he said quietly, holding on to her as he rolled onto his back, ceding her the power now. She kissed his chin, his chest, pushing herself slowly down the length of his body, her fingertips tracing his every muscle, all the fascinating ridges and small valleys that made up his personal landscape.

She didn't have Sam's expertise, really wasn't sure what he'd like, how to please him, but what she lacked in expertise she hoped would be overshadowed by her very true desire to give back at least some of the pleasure he'd given her. Tentatively, she cupped him in her hands. Tentatively, she kissed him. Dared to touch him with the tip of her tongue.

Above her, she heard Sam sigh her name as he said, "Yes, yes," and she was lost….

Eight

Sam tore up the stairs to his quarters in Balfour Hall, cursing as he went, stripping off his tie as he took the steps two at a time. Late. Late. He was late.

Don't let him be too late....

He'd promised Paige he'd be back in plenty of time, time he needed to explain what couldn't be explained long-distance, during their daily talks on the phone. Those wonderful, long, intimate and sometimes carefully worded talks.

She hadn't told him about her anonymous gift.

He hadn't told her why she'd received it or what tonight was really all about.

He'd decided that was something he had to explain to her face-to-face.

Now he was running out of time. His flight had been delayed because of the weather. He shouldn't have chanced I-95, not at five o'clock. Not with a slick coating of snow slowing the highway to a near crawl and then going to full stop after some jackass with four-wheel drive thought the Caution: Bridge Freezes Before Road Surface sign was meant for everybody but him.

Wealth and reputation had some perks. The private jet from Singapore and little more than a wink and a nod got him through customs. But nobody winked at Mother Nature or could protect you from idiots.

Like himself. When it came to idiots, Sam had decided he just about topped the list. Close the deal with Chang Industries—no problem. Close the deal with Paige? Big problem.

Because first he'd had to close the deal with *himself,* and a lifetime of stupid ideas and conclusions, childhood, childish conclusions that had no place in his adult world.

As Sam stripped and got into the shower, not waiting until the water heated, he cursed himself for the millionth time for not telling Paige the truth, all of the truth, about her gift, his part in it, Uncle Ned, what was going to happen tonight, his private revelations—all of it.

Mostly, he should have told her about Uncle Ned. Definitely. Sweet old Uncle Ned. The *gardener.* Would he actually show up for the party? Of course he would. He wouldn't want to miss the fun of watching his nephew eat three or four straight courses of crow.

Fifteen minutes later, his hair still damp and his bowtie crooked, Sam was back downstairs and heading for the banquet hall.

At least, during one of their phone calls, he'd had the common sense to ask Paige to be here early tonight, to act as his hostess for the dinner party. So she would already be there, wondering where the hell he was.

Sam stopped, pushed up the sleeve of his tuxedo and looked at his wristwatch. "Wrong," he told himself, wincing. "Not wondering. Pacing…and *pissed*."

"I still don't understand why Sam didn't want place cards," Paige said, wringing her hands together as she gave the elaborately set table one last inspection as Mary Sue slid one of the crystal wine glasses a half inch to the right.

"Relax," Mary Sue soothed, although there was a hint of tension in her own voice. "He said *hostess*, right? That means he's at the head of the table and you're at the bottom—the other end. Unless he wants you to sit at his right hand side, of course, because I've read that it's also done that way sometimes. Besides, you're going to knock his socks off when he gets a look at you in that gown, and he'll probably want you to sit on his lap."

Paige smiled, feeling heat run into her cheeks. "I

still think it's too low-cut," she said, touching a hand to her cleavage. "I mean, there's being subtle and then there's *come to mama, big boy*. I think this gown might have crossed the line."

"Okay, I've tried to convince you, in the store when you tried it on, while the gal was wrapping it up and again tonight. Be a prude if you want to, because that's it for me. I'm done. I'm outta here. I've got this kid, and he has this thing about wanting *his* mama home on Christmas Eve. But I'll give it one parting shot, since I know you're really nervous. You look terrific, Paige, like a woman in love, waiting for her man to come home. This place looks terrific. It looked terrific on TV last night, it looked terrific in the magazine and in the newspaper. It's going to look just as terrific next year when Holidays by Halliday is the cover shot seen on every newsstand in America."

"Yeah," Paige said, casting her gaze over the rest of the banquet hall, unable to keep a shiver of excitement from dancing up her spine. "Terrific. Thanks, Mary Sue. And you're right, you should go home now. Sam will be here soon. He landed over two hours ago."

"It's the snow, it held him up. A typical Pennsylvania white Christmas, more trouble than it's worth," Mary Sue said, gathering up her purse and the large canvas satchel stuffed with scissors, tape, glue and anything else that might be needed for a last-minute on-site repair of one of their decorations. "If you guys are lucky, it held up everybody else who's coming, too."

Paige hugged her assistant and kissed her on the cheek. "Thank you, Mary Sue, for everything, and Merry Christmas. Come on, I'll walk you to the door."

They passed by the "village stalls" with their gaily striped canopies, a centerpiece of greens and thick white candles in glass sleeves set on the plank counter of each serving station tonight. During the open house on New Year's Day, those stalls would serve as stations for the lavish buffet, everything served on the newly polished silver plate Mrs. Clarkson had shown her a few days ago. An entire room lined with shelves, each shelf filled with gorgeous antique silver. The job may have been the largest Paige had ever taken on, but it sure had come loaded with materials that couldn't help but give the whole thing that *wow* factor.

"It's a whole other world, this house, isn't it?" Paige asked as they entered the foyer. She stopped, her breath caught yet again by the splendor of this towering space. Uncle Ned had outdone himself with the tall floral centerpiece on the round table and the exotic, weeping greens wrapping up the double staircases filled the room with the smells of Christmas.

"Holy...*whoa*."

Paige tore her gaze from the enormous chandelier almost directly above their heads. It was hung now with dozens of looping strings of real Austrian crystal garland that cast a rainbow of sparkling light everywhere. The fifty-two little ivory shades had been replaced with the red velvet ones Paige had discovered in one of the boxes. Perfect. It was just perfect. But Mary Sue was looking toward the hallway. "What?" she asked. She turned her head, and then froze. "*Sam.*"

"Merry Christmas, Paige," Mary Sue whispered as she quickly slipped into her parka. "Good luck unwrapping *that.*"

It was almost like the first time he'd seen her. She wasn't covered in glitter this time, but she shone like an angel just the same as she stood beneath the chandelier, her gown a slim column of shimmering silver silk. Simple, elegant, whispering sex in its every line and curve and yet entirely classy and classic. Just like her.

"Hello, Paige," Sam said, his legs finally able to move again, so that he could approach her, slip his hands onto her hips. "I've missed you. Very much."

Paige lowered her gaze for a moment and then looked up at him, her eyes shining with what he was afraid were unshed tears. She raised a hand to his cheek as she searched his expression. "I was so afraid of this moment these past two weeks. And…and now it's here."

"And are you still afraid?" Sam asked her, stepping closer to her, pulling her hips gently against his.

Paige slowly shook her head. "No. I don't think I am. You're not going to say goodbye, are you?"

"No, sweetheart. Not this time. Not to you. Not ever."

He lowered his lips to hers, capturing her sigh as she opened her mouth for him. There was passion as he kissed her, as they held each other, but passion was only a part of what Sam felt. He was *home*.

"Come to the library with me," he said moments later against her ear. "We have to talk."

"But your guests will be—"

He grabbed her hand, cutting her off. "I know, Paige. That's why we have to talk now. There's something I have to explain to you before they arrive. I've already put if off too long, hoping to let you go first and—*damn!*"

The sound of the door chimes brought Mrs. Clarkson and her simple black dress into the foyer, where she hesitated with her hand on the latch, looking to Sam. "Will you greet your guests here, sir, or should I wait until you and Ms. Halliday retire to the banquet hall?"

"Just a moment, please, Mrs. Clarkson. Hoping I'd go first with what, Sam?" Paige asked as she reached up to straighten his bowtie. "But it's all right. Your guests come first right now. We can talk later, although you really should see the poinsettia tree. It's gorgeous. I want you to see all the rest of the house, too. Not that you've said anything about this space. I think they nailed it, Uncle Ned and the gang. He was such a huge help. I don't think we would have made it without Uncle Ned."

"Yeah, he's always a big help. A regular Santa

Claus." Sam held up his hand toward Mrs. Clarkson, silently telling her to continue to wait. "All right. Just promise me something first, Paige."

"Sam? What's wrong? I thought we were—"

"All right? You thought we were all right? We are. *I* am, and I hope you are. But there are things you don't know about—"

The chimes pealed a second time.

Sam put his hands on Paige's shoulder. "Do you trust me?"

"*Trust* you? Sam?"

"Just trust me. No matter what you hear tonight, no matter how this all goes down—and God only knows what Uncle Ned is planning—just remember that it doesn't matter. Nothing matters here tonight, Paige, except you and me."

"Uncle Ned? What would Uncle Ned be planning? You're scaring me, Sam," Paige said quietly.

"But you'll do it?"

"Trust you, you mean." She nodded. "I will, Sam. I promise."

Sam expelled a breath and dropped his arm, indicating that Mrs. Clarkson could open the door now.

Sam introduced her as "the genius behind these magnificent decorations," as "my very good friend, Paige Halliday."

Paige listened closely each time he introduced her to a new arrival, wondering what she hoped to hear and wasn't hearing. Still, he kept his arm around her waist, kept her close to him as drinks were poured, polite conversation was conducted and a variety of canapés were offered from silver trays.

She stopped counting after three couples had arrived and been introduced, as there would be only one extra place setting at the table, one Sam had already informed her may or may not be needed. If it came time to be seated and their last guest had not yet arrived, the place setting would be removed.

Finally, Mrs. Clarkson came up to quietly say something to Sam, and he went off with her, leaving Paige to circulate without him. She loved the attention he was paying her, the way he kept her beside him, but she was beginning to believe they were joined at the hip—or that he was afraid to let her out of his sight. But if she was the hostess, she needed to mingle more with his invited guests.

Paige accepted the compliments everyone heaped on her, and she explained that there was to be an open house on New Year's Day, and how the tented stalls would be employed as small carving stations, bar setups, and the like.

Emily Raines, a petite blonde with an infectious enthusiasm, actually went so far as to suggest that Paige was an artist. "And, as an artist myself, please let me say that I'm extremely jealous. It takes real vision to take a space this huge and make it seem so…intimate."

"My fiancée knows whereof she speaks, Paige," Cole Preston told her as he put his arm around Emily's shoulders. "You should see what she did with one run-down old building and a big dream."

"And a lot of luck in the form of a great big, anonymous check," Emily said as if reminding him of something. "That's how Libby describes what happened to both of us." When Cole looked at her questioningly, Emily laughed. "Libby Jost, that pretty Sissy Spacek look-alike you were manfully trying not to ogle a minute ago. Five minutes together in a powder room, darling, fixing our lipstick, and we women can cover a lot of ground. Besides, we're all pretty sure we know why we're here. To meet our mysterious benefactor. I'm just so happy that I can finally thank him."

Paige smiled as Emily and Cole went on to talk about her arts center for senior citizens and then drifted off to speak with the Sissy Spacek look-alike. But a thought had begun to form in her mind, and her heart was racing in her chest.

Libby and her fiancé, David Halstrom, were deep in conversation with the third couple, a very distinguished and yet devastatingly handsome doctor, Seth Andrews, and his bride, Becca. Paige hesitated to interrupt, but Becca quickly motioned for her to join them.

"Isn't this exciting?" Becca asked Paige. "You know, all three of us—six of us, really—have been wondering since the day our gifts arrived just who could be so very kind, so very giving. And then we got those invitations? I can't tell you how nervous I am."

"Nervous about meeting our reclusive billionaire Santa Claus," Libby Jost clarified, and her fiancé shook his head.

"Excuse her, please, Paige. She saw some gossip column about there being a Santa Claus somewhere out there who rewards the good or the true, or something like that."

"It was in Leticia Trent's 'This 'N' That' gossip column, and when I checked on the Internet, I learned that she's been writing about this Santa Claus for a long time now."

"Which, of course, makes it all fact," David said, winking at Paige. "Or do you know something we don't know? Sam seems like a nice guy, and this place is certainly impressive. But he doesn't look much like a Santa Claus."

Paige kept her smile, even as her stomach dropped to her toes. "Um…exactly what does this Santa do, please? I'm afraid I don't quite understand."

Libby happily explained as Emily and Cole joined them. According to Leticia Trent, some anonymous billionaire (Sam? He qualified, Paige supposed) picked people to present with a gift, monetary or otherwise, to reward them for something generous and unselfish that they'd done. If the person kept the gift, used it the way ninety-nine percent of people probably would—for themselves—that was the end of the story.

"But," David told her, "if the person uses the gift for the good of others, then there is another gift. According to this Trent woman, that gift is one million tax-free dollars."

"*What?* I mean—pardon me?" Paige shot her gaze around the banquet hall, madly searching for Sam. Who she was pretty sure she then planned to kill. Slowly.

"It's all rumor, gossip. But, if it *is* true, David and I have already decided not to keep it. Not that you guys have to do something like that, of course. It's just what we decided, once I read the articles."

Dr. Seth Andrews looked at Becca. "This is…interesting. Isn't it? I only thought we would be meeting the anonymous giver tonight. We didn't plan on anything so bizarre, did we, sweetheart? I don't know that I want to stick around for this."

Becca only sighed. "Don't go all proud on me, Cole Preston. Somebody did a very nice thing, and I want to thank him." She turned to Paige. "Besides, I highly doubt the man is going to play Santa to the tune of three million tax-free dollars. That story is nothing but sensationalistic gossip. It has to be."

"Yes, of course. I'm sure that's all it is," Paige agreed and then mumbled an excuse about needing to check on some last-minute details before they sat down to dinner.

Her smile left her face the moment she'd turned her back on the six guests, and her eyelids narrowed as she searched the shadows of the large room for any sign of Sam. Who, if he had a brain in his head, was hiding somewhere.

All the pieces were falling into place for her now. Sam was—Paige closed her eyes for a moment— *Sam*-ta Claus. *He* had written that letter he'd delivered. *He* had set up this whole thing, *investigating* her, monitoring what she'd done with his anonymous gift, hiring her to decorate his house, watching her like a bug under a microscope to see how she'd react, which way she'd jump.

It was sickening.

Disgusting.

Maybe even a little bit creepy.

Except…

It was also a new van for the kids at Lark Summit. It was a great art center for senior citizens in Kansas. It was expanding a health clinic in West Virginia and a wonderful children's park in Missouri.

And none of it sounds anything like the Sam Balfour I know, Paige told herself as she turned around once more, just in time to see everyone else looking at Sam, who had asked for everyone's kind attention.

She watched as he sought her out with his rather troubled-looking brown eyes, and she fought not to turn on her heels and run out of the banquet hall. But he'd asked her to trust him, so at least she could listen to whatever it was he had to say.

He'd better start talking, though. Fast.

"I want to thank you all for honoring your invitations and coming here tonight," he said, and then smiled. "Not that it wasn't a command request, was it? I'm sorry about that. By now I'm sure you've all compared notes enough to know that you've all been the recipients of anonymous gifts this year, and you may even think you've been invited here tonight to thank your benefactor. But that's not why you're here. You're here so that your benefactor can thank *you*. You've made him very proud, warmed his heart and, although it pains me to admit this, shown me how right he is and how wrong I was. You are, all of you, quite remarkable human beings. Some might even say you're members of a vanishing breed, although your benefactor doesn't believe that."

Paige wet her lips, wishing her throat hadn't gone so dry. Sam looked quite imposing, and his speech, the genuine humbleness in his voice, made her feel that she didn't really know him at all.

"There will be lawyers and legal formalities later, I'm afraid, necessary forms covering the confidentiality of this evening. But for now, let me say that each of you four recipients—Libby, Becca, Emily…and Paige—out of many who received similar anonymous gifts during the course of this year, have earned not only your benefactor's admiration, but also tax-free checks in the amount of one million dollars."

There was a gasp from one of the women, and Paige heard a whispered "I *told* you so" from Libby.

"In the normal course of events," Sam went on, "your benefactor would still be anonymous, but I was fortunate enough to convince him that, after many years of, as some people may call it, playing Santa Claus, it was time he came out of the shadows and met the people he so admires. And so, ladies and gentleman, please allow me to introduce my uncle, Samuel Edward Balfour IV."

As Sam gestured toward the far archway, Paige turned along with everyone else, to see…

"Uncle Ned?"

His silver hair shining in the light of several dozen candles and the crystal chandeliers, his smile brighter than any of them, dressed in a wonderfully fitting tuxedo rather than overalls and a plaid flannel shirt, Uncle Ned walked into the large room, stopped, sought out Paige with his twinkling eyes and waved rather sheepishly in her direction.

Paige slowly shook her head even as she began to move backward, away from the facts that had just been flung in her face. "No…no…"

She turned and ran toward the foyer.

"Paige! Paige—wait! Damn it, Paige, you promised you'd trust me."

Paige skidded to a halt in the middle of the great foyer, remembering that her coat and purse were in the library and that it was snowing outside. She wasn't going anywhere, so she might as well have her say. She whirled around to face him.

"And you promised me that…that you'd—oh, forget it! You didn't promise me anything, did you? You gave me your line, and I just folded like a house of cards. You and your uncle, the both of you. Just lie after lie after lie. You're a real pair, and I'm a real jerk!"

"I should have told you sooner," Sam said, approaching her carefully, as if she might bolt at any moment, just open the front door and go running out into the snow. "I was wrong. I know that. I wanted to tell you. But Uncle Ned wants to be anonymous… wanted to be anonymous. And you never said anything. I kept hoping you'd feel you could tell me on your own, but you didn't."

Paige looked away, hating that he was actually making at least some sense. She could have told him. She just hadn't. "I was worried the van might be involved in something illegal."

Sam smiled—and she longed to hit him. She loved him, but that didn't mean he wasn't ripe for a good right cross, darn it! "Illegal, Paige? Still? How could the van be illegal?"

"I don't know! I said money laundering, but that didn't make sense. Nothing made sense. And you said you were acting only as a delivery person for a client, or something like that. How could I tell you what your client wouldn't tell you? *Especially* if there was something weird going on with the whole thing. Because I wasn't going to have you tell me that I needed to give the van back, Sam. Those children need that van. So I…I just tried to put the entire thing out of my mind and forget it had ever happened."

"And now you're angry because you're one million dollars richer?"

"Yes! No!" She scrubbed at her face with her hand, without a thought to her makeup. "I mean, I'll just give it to Lark Summit. I make my own way in life, I always have."

"But you never forget where you came from," Sam said, edging even closer.

She looked at him intensely. "You—Uncle Ned— you had me investigated, didn't you? You probably know more about me than I know about me."

"I know what you are, Paige. A good person. Not a do-gooder. You're so much more than that. You're like my father, although I didn't realize why I was so angry with him or why I was fighting buying into Uncle Ned's beliefs. You're a good person who does good things."

She shook her head. "No, that's not right. I mean, not about your father, but about me. Don't try to fit me with a halo, Sam. I'm a selfish person. I give to Lark Summit, decorate the residence for holidays and things like that, because I'm a *selfish* person. I like the way I feel when I'm helping those kids."

"We'll argue some more later." He reached out and took her hand. "Come on, let's go to the library while Uncle Ned covers for us. I want to see that poinsettia tree."

Paige let him guide her back through the house to the library, where the poinsettia tree, backlit with spotlights half buried in the snow outside, stood as her favorite decoration out of anything she'd done. "It's beautiful, isn't it?"

"It's just the way I remember it," Sam said, leaning in to kiss her cheek. "Thank you, Paige. You can think what you want, and I'm certain you will, but you've made a huge difference in my life, and in Uncle Ned's. When I started this, I had no idea how it would end up, but that's what happened. Uncle Ned would say, undoubtedly will say, that I've finally grown up. So stay or go, that's entirely up to you, but please let me say this first. I love you, Paige. I love you, and I want you in my life if you'll have me. Now and for the rest of our lives."

If there was one thing Paige had learned growing up "in the system" it was how to choose her battles, when to fight and when it was simply easier to give in and go along with the inevitable.

Sam was inevitable.

"Oh, Sam…"

"I know this is happening quickly for you. It is for me, too. But when I saw you standing under that chandelier in the great foyer? My first thought was, my God, I love that woman. My next thought was that there should be children sitting together on the steps behind you, allowed to stay up late and watch their beautiful mother and their proud father as they hosted their annual Christmas Eve reception. For a moment, Paige, the image was so clear in my head that I had to stop and remember that it wasn't real. But it could be. If you can forgive me for being such a—"

Paige put her hand over his mouth. "Too much talking, Sam. Much, much too much talking. Please, just shut up and kiss me…."

Epilogue

Sam and Paige entered Uncle Ned's private study. They were still smiling about the way Sam had carried her across the threshold of their own quarters a few minutes early, and then had nearly dropped her when a startled maid who was vacuuming the foyer carpet shrieked in surprise and tried to pull the vacuum cleaner out of the foyer with her—the cord catching at Sam's ankles.

As Sam had said, that would show them to cut their honeymoon short and come back two days early, unannounced. But Easter would arrive in three weeks, and an apologetic Mary Sue had phoned to say that Paul had fallen off a ladder while stretching to reach a four-foot-high Easter egg that had been the second straight purple one in a row of suspended eggs that was supposed to alternate between purple and yellow. Now Paul was purple, black and blue and even turning a little yellow in spots, and Paige was needed back on the job at Holidays by Halliday, ASAP.

"Sam! Paige! You're home," Uncle Ned exclaimed, waving them into his presence like some king who must be obeyed. "You look wonderful, both of you. How was the honeymoon? How was Barbados?"

"Come with us next time, Uncle Ned, and find out for yourself," Sam told him as Paige crossed over to the desk to give the older man a hug and kiss. "You did promise us you'd stop staying cooped up in here, remember?"

"I'll have you two know that I commandeered Bruce, and we went for a drive just the other day." He looked up at Paige. "To Lark Summit. It seems they'd like a baseball field."

"Yes," Paige said, smiling at Sam. "I know."

"And did you know that Bruce once played semipro ball, Sam? He's not only agreed to help with the planning but has also volunteered to help coach."

"Really? Does that mean you're not going to have him running all over the country investigating people for your Santa project anymore, hiding behind trees and invading people's privacy, as Paige described it?"

"I'm afraid there's no more Santa project. You were right, Sam. That Trent woman was getting too close. Part of the joy Maureen and I got over the years was being anonymous, and if that is lost to me, why not simply go completely public? Paige, there will be papers for you to sign in a few weeks, but I'd be greatly pleased if you'll help me run the Maureen Balfour Foundation. If part of the fun for us came from being anonymous, the greatest majority of our satisfaction was in the giving itself."

Paige hugged the man again. "I'd be honored, Uncle Ned. Thank you so much." Then she leaned past him, to pick up a newspaper clipping on the desktop. "What's this? Isn't that—Sam, look. It's a photograph of Libby Jost."

Sam took the clipping from her and read the caption out loud. "'Plans were announced today for a proposed major addition to the newest children's park in the area. Libby Jost, seen here presenting a check for one million dollars to Mayor Cliff Hagen, says the money is earmarked for the construction of a one-of-a-kind carousel and other improvements. The hope is that renting the carousel and an adjoining building for parties will supply a steady income for the park.'"

"It's the last entry for my scrapbook, at least for this one," Uncle Ned said when Sam handed back the clipping. "Emily Raines has underwritten two more senior citizen art centers in towns not far from her original project. And Becca and her new husband, as you know, immediately donated her check to that same clinic in West Virginia. Now we begin a new scrapbook, Paige, and fill it with bouquets to my Maureen."

"Oh, Uncle Ned, that's the perfect name for the foundation."

"And what's my job, Uncle Ned?" Sam asked as Paige came around to the front of the desk, to slip an arm around his waist. "Or do I just get to watch?"

Uncle Ned blinked up at his nephew. "I didn't think you'd want to become involved in—do you really want to help, Sam? From your heart?"

"From my heart, Uncle Ned. I can't think of anything I'd like to do more, from my heart. Except kiss my bride, that is."

So he did.

* * * * *

One

Hunter Cabot, Navy SEAL, had a healing bullet wound in his side, thirty days' leave and, apparently, a wife he'd never met.

On the drive into his hometown of Springville, California, he stopped for gas at Charlie Evans's service station. That's where the trouble started.

"Hunter! Man, it's good to see you! Margie didn't tell us you were coming home."

"Margie?" Hunter leaned back against the front fender of his black pickup truck and winced as his side gave a small twinge of pain. Silently then, he watched as the man he'd known since high school filled his tank.

Charlie grinned, shook his head and pumped gas. "Guess your wife was lookin' for a little 'alone' time with you, huh?"

"My—" Hunter couldn't even say the word. *Wife?* He didn't have a wife. "Look, Charlie..."

"Don't blame her, of course," his friend said with a wink as he finished up and put the gas cap back on. "You being gone all the time with the SEALs must be hard on the ol' love life."

He'd never had any complaints, Hunter thought, frowning at the man still talking a mile a minute. "What're you—"

"Bet Margie's anxious to see you. She told us all about that R and R trip you two took to Bali." Charlie's dark brown eyebrows lifted and wiggled.

"Charlie..."

"Hey, it's okay, you don't have to say a thing, man."

What the hell could he say? Hunter shook his head, paid for his gas and as he left, told himself Charlie was just losing it. Maybe the guy had been smelling gas fumes too long.

But as it turned out, it wasn't just Charlie. Stopped at a red light on Main Street, Hunter glanced out his window to smile at Mrs. Harker, his second-grade teacher who was now at least a hundred years old. In the middle of the crosswalk, the old lady stopped and shouted, "Hunter Cabot, you've got yourself a wonderful wife. I hope you appreciate her."

Scowling now, he only nodded at the old woman—the only teacher who'd ever scared the crap out of him. What the hell was going on here? Was everyone but him nuts?

His temper beginning to boil, he put up with a few more comments about his "wife" on the drive through town before finally pulling into the wide, circular drive leading to the Cabot mansion. Hunter didn't have a clue what was going on, but he planned to get to the bottom of it. Fast.

He grabbed his duffel bag, stalked into the house and paid no attention to the housekeeper, who ran at him, fluttering both hands. "Mr. Hunter!"

"Sorry, Sophie," he called out over his shoulder as he took the stairs two at a time. "Need a shower, then we'll talk."

He marched down the long, carpeted hallway to the rooms that were always kept ready for him. In his suite, Hunter tossed the duffel down and stopped dead. The shower in his bathroom was running. His *wife?*

Anger and curiosity boiled in his gut, creating a churning mass that had him moving forward without even thinking about it. He opened the bathroom door to a wall of steam and the sound of a woman singing—off-key. Margie, no doubt.

Well, if she was his wife...Hunter walked across the room, yanked the shower door open and stared in at a curvy, naked, temptingly wet woman.

She whirled to face him, slapping her arms across her naked body while she gave a short, terrified scream.

Hunter smiled. "Hi, honey. I'm home."

* * * * *

Be sure to look for
AN OFFICER AND A MILLIONAIRE
by USA TODAY *bestselling author Maureen Child.*
Available January 2009 from Silhouette Desire.

CELEBRATE
60 YEARS
OF PURE READING PLEASURE
WITH HARLEQUIN®!

We'll be spotlighting a different series
every month throughout 2009
to celebrate our 60th anniversary.
Look for Silhouette Desire® in January!

MAN of the
MONTH

Collect all 12 books in the Silhouette Desire®
Man of the Month continuity, starting in
January 2009 with *An Officer and a Millionaire*
by *USA TODAY* bestselling author
Maureen Child.

*Look for one new Man of the Month title
every month in 2009!*

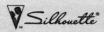

REQUEST YOUR FREE BOOKS!

2 FREE NOVELS
PLUS 2
FREE GIFTS!

Passionate, Powerful, Provocative!

YES! Please send me 2 FREE Silhouette Desire® novels and my 2 FREE gifts (gifts are worth about $10). After receiving them, if I don't wish to receive any more books, I can return the shipping statement marked "cancel". If I don't cancel, I will receive 6 brand-new novels every month and be billed just $4.05 per book in the U.S. or $4.74 per book in Canada, plus 25¢ shipping and handling per book and applicable taxes, if any*. That's a savings of almost 15% off the cover price! I understand that accepting the 2 free books and gifts places me under no obligation to buy anything. I can always return a shipment and cancel at any time. Even if I never buy another book, the two free books and gifts are mine to keep forever.   225 SDN ERVX 326 SDN ERVM

Name	(PLEASE PRINT)	
Address		Apt. #
City	State/Prov.	Zip/Postal Code

Signature (if under 18, a parent or guardian must sign)

Mail to the Silhouette Reader Service:
IN U.S.A.: P.O. Box 1867, Buffalo, NY 14240-1867
IN CANADA: P.O. Box 609, Fort Erie, Ontario L2A 5X3

Not valid to current subscribers of Silhouette Desire books.

Want to try two free books from another line?
Call 1-800-873-8635 or visit www.morefreebooks.com.

* Terms and prices subject to change without notice. N.Y. residents add applicable sales tax. Canadian residents will be charged applicable provincial taxes and GST. Offer not valid in Quebec. This offer is limited to one order per household. All orders subject to approval. Credit or debit balances in a customer's account(s) may be offset by any other outstanding balance owed by or to the customer. Please allow 4 to 6 weeks for delivery. Offer available while quantities last.

Your Privacy: Silhouette Books is committed to protecting your privacy. Our Privacy Policy is available online at www.eHarlequin.com or upon request from the Reader Service. From time to time we make our lists of customers available to reputable third parties who may have a product or service of interest to you. If you would prefer we not share your name and address, please check here. ☐

SDES08R

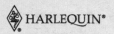

You're invited to join our Tell Harlequin Reader Panel!

By joining our new reader panel you will:

- Receive Harlequin® books—they are FREE and yours to keep with no obligation to purchase anything!
- Participate in fun online surveys
- Exchange opinions and ideas with women just like you
- Have a say in our new book ideas and help us publish the best in women's fiction

In addition, you will have a chance to win great prizes and receive special gifts! See Web site for details. Some conditions apply. Space is limited.

To join, visit us at

www.TellHarlequin.com.

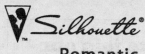

Silhouette® Romantic SUSPENSE

Sparked by Danger, Fueled by Passion.

Justine Davis

Baby's Watch

THE COLTONS
~FAMILY FIRST~

Former bad boy Ryder Colton has never felt a connection to much, so he's shocked when he feels one to the baby he helps deliver, and her mother. Ana Morales doesn't quite trust this stranger, but when her daughter is taken by a smuggling ring, she teams up with him in the hope of rescuing her baby. With nowhere to turn she has no choice but to trust Ryder with her life...and her heart.

Available January 2009 wherever books are sold.

Look for the final installment of
the Coltons: Family First miniseries,
A Hero of Her Own by Carla Cassidy in February 2009.

COMING NEXT MONTH

#1915 AN OFFICER AND A MILLIONAIRE—
Maureen Child
Man of the Month
A naval officer returns home to discover he's married…to a woman he's never even met!

#1916 BLACKMAILED INTO A FAKE ENGAGEMENT—
Leanne Banks
The Hudsons of Beverly Hills
It started as a PR diversion, but soon their pretend engagement leads to real passion. Could their Hollywood tabloid stunt actually turn into true love?

#1917 THE EXECUTIVE'S VALENTINE SEDUCTION—
Merline Lovelace
Holidays Abroad
Determined to atone for past sins, he would enter into a marriage of convenience and leave his new wife set for life. But a romantic Valentine's Day in Spain could change his plans.…

#1918 MAN FROM STALLION COUNTRY—
Annette Broadrick
The Crenshaws of Texas
A forbidden passion throws a couple into the ultimate struggle— between life and love.

#1919 THE DUKE'S BOARDROOM AFFAIR—
Michelle Celmer
Royal Seductions
This charming, handsome duke had never met a woman he couldn't seduce—until now. Though his new assistant sees right through him, he's made it his business to get her into his bed!

#1920 THE TYCOON'S PREGNANT MISTRESS—
Maya Banks
The Anetakis Tycoons
Months after tossing his mistress out of his life, he discovers she has amnesia—and is pregnant with his child! Pretending they're engaged, he strives to gain her love *before* she remembers.…

SDCNMBPA1208